Hands On

More Than Friends #5

Aria Grace

Hands On

Published by Surrendered Press

Chapter One

CALEB

When a shot glass is slammed on the table in front of me, sloshing tequila all over the Applied General Equilibrium Economics book I've been staring at for an hour, I know this is gonna be a shitty night. I've already had two tricks and it's not even eight thirty. I really need to study but I also need to make some cash.

I casually wipe the pages of my book with my sleeve and paste on my sexiest smile. I'm a professional and the sooner I graduate, the sooner I can stop peddling my ass and get a real job.

One look at the dirty Carhartts to my right and I know who the drink is from. Ron is becoming a regular but I'm not sure if that's a good thing. He can be cool when he's just drinking beer but tonight he's hit the tequila.

"Ron, hey." I lean back and push out the chair next to me with my foot. "Have a seat."

"Hey, baby." He drops heavily into the chair and looks at me from under his Seahawks hat. "You got a few minutes for me?"

"I always have time for you." I start stacking my books and glance at the clock above the register. "You ready now or do you want to finish your drink?"

"That's for you, baby." He scoots the shot closer as he lifts his own. "We'll drink together."

There's no way in hell I'm drinking anything he dropped in front of me. Especially not before going upstairs alone with him. I haven't known him for more than a few weeks so I need to stay alert.

"You're so sweet but I can't drink tonight." I pat the stack of books with my left hand as I scoot the glass to Ron. "I have to study tonight but I can wait while you finish both."

As the words come out, I know how stupid they are. He's obviously already had several. Two more shots are not going to make this night easier but it's too late now.

Ron just shakes his head as he pounds both shots in two breaths. His face pinches slightly but he's past the point of tasting it. I feel a slight shudder just witnessing it. I'd be puking by now if I tried that shit.

"You need to loosen up, kid." He stands and sways for a second, steading himself on the back of the chair. "You've always got your fucking nose buried in a book."

He's right. I try to look embarrassed by it but I'm not. I've worked hard to put myself through community college and I plan to transfer to Portland State in the fall. If I want to graduate within the next two years, I can't be getting drunk with frat boys every night.

I've spent the last two and a half years in this bar seven nights a week. When I'm not on Ray's payroll building drinks, I'm on my own payroll working tricks upstairs.

I'm not ashamed of where I'm at or how I got here. But I am eager to move past this point in my life. Just because my parents didn't want to watch their fairy son graduate from college or grow into a man, doesn't mean I'm not going to make it happen on my own. It does, however, mean I need to get through this fucking advanced equilibrium econ class and not get drunk tonight.

"I know." I stand and reach for his hand. He bypasses it and slides his arm around my waist instead, pulling me into his side forcefully. "But this is how I have fun."

As soon as we're alone in the office Ray allows me to use for tricks, Ron gets handsy. His beefy fingers close around the back of my neck and he guides me to the leather sofa. "I want you raw tonight, sweetheart."

I still under his hand. I don't do raw. Ever. I may have sex for money but I've never once had so much as a broken rubber. I'm clean and I intend to stay that way.

"You know I can't do that, Ron. I'd love to feel you inside me but Ray would cut me off if he found out." I turn up the charm and try to reason with him. "But I've got the magnum extra-large that I know you need. It'll still be tight on you but that'll just make it feel even better."

The buffoon buys my fake flattery and loosens his grip on my neck. "It better be fuckin huge because I've been rockin a goddamn log since I walked in."

He's not exceptionally well endowed but he's a man and he likes to be told his dick is big. Since he's paying me, I give him what his delicate ego needs. Reaching for his crotch, I smile. "Mmm, that's gonna feel so good."

"Fuck yeah it is." He thrusts into my hand. "Get it."

I guess we're done with the bedroom talk. With my hands under his shirt, I nudge him to the sofa. He falls into the middle of it and spreads his legs wide as he throws his head back, letting his arms rest on the cushions to either side of him.

I drop to my knees and unbutton his pants. If I don't move quick, he'll probably pass out. As much as I wouldn't mind if he did, I don't want to leave his two hundred pound ass up here all night while he sleeps it off so I need to get him in and out, literally, as soon as possible.

Once his dick is released from his jeans, his hand is back around my neck. Ron only allows me a few seconds to pull the condom from my pocket and get it in place before he's bucking into my mouth. I try to just relax and take it but his grip is tight, causing my whole body to tense.

I know fighting it isn't going to help but I can't stop myself from trying to pull off. Of course, he isn't having any of that. Ron gets off on the panicked look in my eyes and smiles as I twist my shoulders, trying to get air into my burning lungs.

"That's it, baby. Take it good." His other hand rakes across the top of my head until the heel of his palm is at my forehead. He curls his fingers, tugging my fine hair into the sweaty crevices of his hand. Normally, I like to have my hair pulled a little bit but between the pain on my neck and the extended periods between each breath, I go into full-on panic mode.

My jaw instinctively clenches and I bite the base of Ron's cock. Hard. His fist rips my head away from him and he swings my whole body to the ground. "What the fuck, Caleb. You think that shit is funny?"

He grabs the front of my shirt and lifts me straight up then tosses me onto the couch.

"I'm sorry, babe. I didn't mean to." I turn my head into my shoulder to rub my stinging eyes. "I couldn't breathe for a minute there and I think my survival instincts kicked in."

He's lucky I didn't bite that shit off.

I smile and pretend my breathlessness is lust-induced as I reach for him. "Let me make it up to you."

He looks around the room for a second like he's not sure how to respond. Finally, he exhales loudly then seems to get back into it. When his softening dick starts to fill up, I know we're back in business. I sit up and run my fingers down his arm and across his belly. "Just lay back and I'll do all the work."

"Uh uh." He grabs the waistband of my jeans and pulls me up. "Take these off and bend over the side."

Trying to keep my smile sexy instead of disgusted, I unzip my skinny jeans and push them down to my ankles. I don't usually wear underwear so once I step out and yank my shirt off, I'm fully bare to Ron.

"That's right, baby." He runs a finger over my nipple then down to the tip of my dick. "You're gonna like this."

I'm semi hard. Not enough to prove actual interest in him but enough to prove I'm a virile man of twenty-three and can keep it up for as long as I need to. "How do you want me?"

Without actual words, he grunts and positions me on all fours across the sofa. My head is hanging over the armrest, just waiting for his intrusion.

"Lube's on the table, baby." I left it out earlier and hope he'll be generous. I haven't been fucked in a few days and I know I'm tighter than I like to be with guys like Ron. Guys that like it rough. Most guys come in for a quick blow job and are on their way but Ron is gonna make me earn my hundred bucks tonight.

"The rubber has enough." He pokes a few fingers inside me for about five seconds before they are replaced by his dry dick. "You want me to wear this shit, you must like the way they feel."

I bite my lip and squeeze my eyes shut as he pounds into me. Dry. This will be the last time that fucker touches me. I'll play nice tonight but I'll let Tony know to keep him away from me. Tony is the big ass bar manager on the floor most nights I'm here and is like the brother I've never had.

Once Ron is fully seated inside me, his hands wrap around my waist and dig into my skin. I'm gonna have bruises on both sides but at least that pain is a small distraction from the fire shooting through me as my skin tears with each thrust.

I feel like he's been riding me for an hour but it's probably only been a few minutes before he picks up his pace. Since there is less friction, I have to assume my blood is acting as lube and I'm thankful when he finally shoots his load. I just pray that condom didn't break with the abuse it's endured because I don't trust this mother fucker as far as I could throw him.

"You always feel so good, baby." Ron is gentle now as he pulls out and tosses the messy condom on the floor. "I could do this every day."

Over my dead body.

"Um hmm..." I carefully slide out from under him and grab my jeans. "That was amazing."

He wants to cuddle but I manage to get dressed. "Can I at least buy you a drink now?"

"I wish I could." I hand him his pants and pick up our trash. Wrapping everything in a few tissues, I drop it in waste basket under the table. "Maybe next time."

Ron stands and reaches for his wallet. "Here's a little extra for taking it like a champ."

He gives me a wet kiss as he slips a few bills in my hand. I don't bother to look at them as I tuck the cash into my back pocket. Turning toward the cabinet where I keep a container of Lysol wipes, I say over my shoulder, "Thanks, Ron. I've got to clean up in here before I head down."

"See you in a few days, baby."

I don't look back until I hear his heavy steps moving down the staircase.

Chapter Two

Patton

I'm just pulling a microwave lasagna out of the freezer when my phone rings. It's Finn. I debate whether or not to answer but I know he'll keep calling until I do. On the third ring, I pick it up.

"Hello." As much as I try to sound pleasant, I know my voice is just annoyed.

"Oh, Patton, hey. I'm glad I caught you." He doesn't sound glad. He sounds disappointed that he can't just leave a message.

"Uh, Finn? Is that you?" He doesn't need to know that I'd never forget his voice. That it haunts my dreams and still stars in all my fantasies. "What's up?"

"I need a favor." Of course he does. Why else would he call me? When he dumped me for the drummer in our band—my band—he made it very clear I wasn't what he wanted anymore.

"And what's that?" I hate myself for even asking. I shouldn't be considering helping this asshole in any way. Not after the way he broke my heart. I thought the distance between us was because he was working longer hours, maybe saving up for a ring or something, but I was naïve. He was working on Jack.

If I learned nothing else from my time with Finn, at least I'll never give my heart so fully and freely to someone that I don't completely know and trust.

"I'm applying for a job at the court house and I need you to be a reference. They want people that have known me for more than two years. Just tell them how responsible I am and that you'd totally hire me." He laughs. "You know, lie."

I force a laugh. "Yeah, that would be a lie."

"So you'll do it?"

Seriously? I groan but I can't refuse. He needs a good job and maybe seeing defendants in courtrooms day in and day out will help set him on a better path in life. "I guess."

"Thanks, man." He's quiet for a second then remembers to ask about me. "So how are things out in Portland? Rain enough for you?"

Just because it doesn't rain that much in Colorado Springs doesn't make it a better conversation starter. But, at least he's trying. "Things are great. I'm working at a nice spa and have met a few people. I love it here."

See, I can lie with the best of them. Truth is, I haven't really met anyone except the single mom that lives downstairs and the girls at work. Everyone's been nice enough but there isn't anyone that I'd actually call a friend.

"Good to hear it." He sounds distracted and there's rustling around on the line. "Okay, I'll let you go. Thanks, man."

"Yeah. Bye."

I shouldn't have a pit in my stomach just from talking to him. I want to be over Finn. I need to be over Finn. But despite the months that have passed and the knowledge that he's clearly moved on without a backward glance, I still want to cry.

No more of this whiney shit, Patton!

I put the Lean Cuisine back in the freezer and head to my room. I'm going out tonight. There's a bar Heather told me about that I've been wanting to check out. No reason why tonight shouldn't be the night.

After a quick shower and a power bar, I head over to Ray's. Heather, the woman that lives below me with her year old daughter, said it's a quiet spot to shoot some pool or just have a drink. That's exactly what I need.

When I walk in, I'm surprised how busy it is for seven PM on a Wednesday. Pop music is playing in the background and several groups of people are seated at tables around the place. There are some open high tops but I don't want to sit alone.

A stool in the middle of the bar seems innocuous enough so I slip onto it and take a look around. This doesn't look like most of the gay bars I've been to but they're definitely gay-friendly, if the small rainbow flag above the register is any indicator. It's actually the only indicator.

Most of the patrons are guys but that's true in most bars. Regardless, I'm not here to pick up anyone. That's not my style. I'm just here for a drink and to feel like a regular guy again. I've missed not having the guys from the band to have a drink with on weekends or after gigs.

By the time I turn back around, the bartender is standing in front of me. "Can I get you something?"

"Tanqueray and Tonic, please."

He smiles and nods. "You got it."

With what I hope isn't taken as anything more than polite curiosity, I watch the kid reach for the bottle from the top shelf. His shirt pulls up slightly, revealing the creamy white skin of his slender hips, peeking out from his dark, tight jeans. The boy looks young—younger than he must be if he's a pouring drinks, but hot.

I'm still staring when he turns around and pours the liquor into a highball. I slowly let my gaze crawl up his chest to his face. He's not looking at me so I study his delicate features and streaked blond hair. It's not too short but you can tell he likes to look good and puts effort into it.

The time he takes is well spent. He's hot as hell. When I glance at him, his crystal blue eyes are trained on me. I want to look away but I can't. He winks then hands me the glass. "Here ya go. That'll be eight bucks."

I pull out a ten and hand it to the kid. When he tries to give me my change, I just shake my head and take a sip. The citrusy drink is smooth and only briefly reminds me of Finn.

As I nurse my drink, I can't help but watch the sexy bartender. He has an easy smile and an infectious laugh. He's clearly liked by all his customers and enjoys chatting them up. Every now and then I catch his eye and he smiles, but then he glances down to my glass to see if I'm ready for a refill. When I finally finish my drink, he's in front of me before the glass meets the wood.

"Ready for another?" He's wiping out the inside of a glass as he waits for my answer.

"Um, yeah." I slide the empty glass to him. "Just one more. I don't usually drink much on work nights."

He nods turns to grab the bottle of Tanqueray. "That's usually a good policy."

He moves gracefully as he prepares my drink. Since I've spent the past thirty minutes watching the poor guy, I've noticed he rolls his shoulders and stretches his neck often.

Before he slides my drink to me, I lay down another ten.

He pulls two singles from the register and tries to hand them to me but I just shake my head. "Keep it."

"Thanks." He drops them into a jar on the back wall and comes back to me. "I haven't seen you in before. Just visiting?"

I take a drink before responding. "New to town. I've only been in the area for a few months."

"Cool." His hand moves to his left shoulder and he rubs circles while nodding slowly. "Where are you from?"

"Colorado." I watch his hand move from his shoulder to his neck. "You got a kink?"

"Oh, yeah." He drops his hand self-consciously. "Occupational hazard."

I look left and right, confused by the comment. "I didn't realize bartending was so dangerous."

He gives me another wink. "It can be."

A guy leans in on my right and places his elbow on the bar beside me, brushing against my back. I bristle at the unexpected contact and lean away.

"Caleb, can you send a couple Cokes to the back when you get a chance?" The man is large with full tattoo sleeves on both arms. He looks like a body builder so I don't look too closely. If he's straight, he probably won't appreciate me checking him out.

"You got it, Steve," Caleb responds.

Caleb. I like it. He looks like a Caleb.

"Thanks, gorgeous." The man drops a twenty on the counter and walks away.

I let out a low whistle. "Damn, Cokes are expensive in here."

He laughs and rings up the drinks then drops the 300% tip in the jar. "He's a good friend."

"I see." If that guy is calling him gorgeous and leaving tips like that, I'm sure he's more than just a friend.

Caleb gives me smirk that tells me he knows what I'm thinking. I hope my snide comment didn't sound as petty as it could have.

When Caleb walks away to place the Cokes on a tray, I turn in my stool and look around again. It's gotten a little busier but I can still see to the billiard tables in the back. The guy, Steve, is playing with a young blond that looks even younger than Caleb. This kid is barely legal. But by the way they watch each other and stop to kiss between almost every shot, it's clear Steve isn't interested in Caleb.

When I spin back around, Caleb is taking a picture of two girls holding up pink drinks at the far end of the bar. When he hands the phone back to them, he notices me watching him. His hand moves to his neck and rubs it while he smiles broadly at me. "Do you need anything else?"

My glass is still half full so I can't use that as an excuse. Besides, I have to work tomorrow and I don't want to feel like shit all day. "No, thanks. But I can probably help with your neck." I take a final drink then stand. "I just started working as a massage therapist at Hydrate Day Spa. Come by and I'll comp a massage."

Caleb takes the card I hand him and looks at it for a minute before understanding dawns. "Oh, my neck." He smiles shyly. "Thanks, I might do that."

CHAPTER THREE

CALEB

Yesterday was bad but I'm even more sore today. Since I woke up this morning, I can't focus on anything but keeping my neck straight. If I wasn't worried about having to answer questions, I would have bought one of those neck rolls people wear for whip lash. But, I don't need the attention so I just sit through four hours of classes and pound Advil every hour.

When I stop in the coffee shop for a sandwich, I see the card that was handed to me last night. Patton Oliver. Massage Therapist. I've never had a massage but if he can do anything to release any of the tension in my neck and shoulders from Ron's rough fuck, I'm tempted to call.

By the time I sit through two more classes, I'm so stiff I can barely think. I call the number on the card and see if Patton has time for a massage today. The receptionist sounds surprised when I ask for Patton by name but assures me he's free at five thirty if I can get there by then. That gives me forty-five minutes. No problem.

When I walk into the downtown salon, I feel self-conscious. It looks a lot like the kind of place my mom would go to get her hair or nails done. I'm about to turn around and walk out when the nice lady behind the counter stops me. "Are you Mr. Forester?"

"Uh, yeah." I turn back around and head to her. "I hope I'm not too early."

"No problem at all." She hands me a clipboard and pen. "Just fill this out then we'll get you settled in."

I sit in the pristine white chair and go through the form. It starts out with standard questions about name and address but when it asks if I'm pregnant or nursing, I glance at the door. I really shouldn't be here. Do guys ever come into this place? It certainly doesn't look like it.

"Is everything okay, sir?" The woman is checking me out with a big smile on her face.

"Yeah, I, uh... Do you get many guys in here?" I walk toward her with the clipboard extended.

"Not too many but that's why we brought in Patton. Having a male massage therapist will make many guys feel more comfortable with coming in here. We've been trying to encourage couples' massages for a while now."

"Okay." I hand her the clipboard. "Well, I guess there's a first for everything."

"You're gonna love it." She hands me a key on a safety pin. "You'll find a robe and slippers in locker four. Just get undressed and Patton will come get you when he's ready."

"Undressed?" Coming straight from school, it never occurred to me that I should run home and shower first. This is awkward.

"It's probably easier to take everything off but if you feel more comfortable with your underwear on, that's fine too."

I nod and try to smile. That would be a great idea if I actually wore underwear. What the hell was I thinking by coming in here?

The locker room is small but the sauna is too tempting so I quickly strip and tie a towel around my waist. If they don't get a lot of men in the spa, I probably don't need to worry about running into anyone else but since I don't know proper etiquette, I keep the towel around my waist as I settle onto the wooden bench.

The dry air immediately relaxes me. I pour some water on the hot rocks and let the blast of heat wash over me. After a few minutes, I force myself to leave the steamy air and hop into the shower.

I feel like a kid in someone else's house as I take a generous dollop of the body wash on the wall and cover myself in it. It smells like cucumbers. Once I use the shampoo and conditioner, I finally dry off and step into the robe. I'm just leaving the shower room when Patton walks in.

"Caleb, hi." He has a broad grin that makes me feel a little less nervous. "I'm glad you decided to come in."

He's even hotter than I remember. In the low lighting at the bar, I couldn't tell just how deep his tan is. He has a golden bronze glow that sets off his longish blond hair perfectly. He reminds me of every guy I crushed on from surfer movies when I was a kid.

He's also taller than I expected. Sitting on a stool, it's almost impossible to tell how tall or short someone is but he's got to be at least six feet. He's only an inch or two taller than me but his broad shoulders and thick biceps flexing under his shirt make me feel tiny by comparison.

"Yeah, I don't know how serious you were but my neck is killing me so I figured it was worth trying a massage."

He places his hand on my elbow and takes a step forward, encouraging me to follow. "I was totally serious. I'm sure I can help at least a little bit."

We walk down a quiet hallway and stop at dark room. Patton motions for me to step inside then he follows me in. "I'll step out for a minute while you take off your robe and get under this sheet."

He pulls back one corner of the white sheet. "Lay face down and I'll be back in a minute."

"Um." I reach for his arm to stop him before he leaves. "I've never done this before so I didn't know what to expect and..."

I can feel my face burning. I should have left when I had the chance.

"And what?" Patton pats my hand, encouraging me to continue.

"Well, I don't usually wear underwear so I'm...naked." I whisper the last word as if someone might hear me and be offended.

His smile is genuine. "Most people are. That's totally fine. I'll make sure you stay covered and if you feel uncomfortable about anything, just let me know. I'm a professional."

I look to the table as Patton ducks out of the room. Once he's gone, I hang the robe on the hook behind the door and neatly slide my slippers under a chair before I get under the sheet.

It takes a second for me to get in a comfortable position and get the sheet back over me but once I do, Patton knocks twice then opens the door. "Are you ready in there?"

"Yeah." I lift my face from the padded donut it's resting in. "Come in."

"Great." His voice is quiet and dim lighting helps put me at ease. I close my eyes and try not to think about the gorgeous man that is about to rub my naked body. "Just relax and we'll get started in just a second."

There's a quiet rustling in the background that almost blends into the sound of waves breaking on a beach. I had a white noise machine when I was a kid and the wave setting was my favorite.

"I'm going to start with light pressure then work into more of a deep tissue. If it's too much pressure or anything hurts, just let me know."

"Okay."

If he takes much longer to start, I'll probably fall asleep. Patton pulls the sheet down so the top half of my back is exposed. The room is warm so I'm not cold but when I hear a fast rubbing sound then feel Patton's hot hands land between my shoulder blades, I think I've died and gone to heaven.

He begins by gently rubbing circles over each shoulder blade. His hands are dry but smooth so they glide over my skin like butter. I don't know if he held his hands over a blazing fire but they leave a burning trail across my shoulders as he increases the pressure.

I don't even realize I've groaned out loud until his hands still. "Is that too much?"

Yes. Too fucking much. Please don't stop.

"No, sorry." I can't believe I'm acting like I've never been touched before. "It feels great."

His hands resume their pattern of kneading and rubbing, though with a little less pressure. He probably thinks I'm a damn pussy.

"I can feel a knot right here." He presses on a tender spot and my body winces away from him. "I can work it out but it'll probably hurt."

"Yeah, that's fine." I don't care what you do as long as you keep your hands on me. "I can take it."

By the time he moves away from the knot in my shoulder, I feel like Jello. The tremendous relief I feel when he moves to my lower back is amazing. Maybe that's the whole point of deep tissue massage. They cause so much pain you feel nothing but joy when it's over.

That might be the case if I actually wanted it to be over. Ever. But I am so aware of Patton's touch on my skin that I want this to go on for hours. And that's before he adds oil to his hands. When his slick hands trail across my lower back, I moan a little again.

Thankfully, he doesn't comment on my reaction. He's a professional and I'm sure he's heard it all.

CHAPTER FOUR

PATTON

When Sarah told me Caleb was here for a massage, I was inappropriately excited. Not just because I've only had two clients all day but because I wanted to see him again.

I had to pace in the break until five twenty-eight so I could give him enough time to get undressed. Just imagining him naked and on my table gave me a semi but I've learned how to disassociate myself from attractive clients.

I didn't spend a small fortune on massage school to become a sexual predator so I remind myself to treat Caleb with the professionalism I'd give to any client and walk into the locker room.

Caleb is just walking out of the shower when I enter the dressing room. His hair is dripping at the ends but he gives me a knee melting smile. I don't even realize how stupid my own grin must look until I catch a glimpse of it in the mirror.

Schooling my features, I reach out to him and tug him forward. When we reach the room we'll be using, I'm nervous as hell. I explain that he should get undressed and try to duck out to control my breathing.

And then he reaches for me. Thank god the lights are dim because when he admits he doesn't normally wear underwear, I know my face is cherry red.

I love hearing content noises from clients but every time Caleb lets out a whimper or soft moan, I feel my dick twitch. Is he vocal in bed? Finn wasn't but based on my body's reaction to Caleb, I think I'd like it.

Then I remember how young Caleb is. He might not be very experienced. Not that I'm Mr. Experience. I've only been with two guys. Sam in college and Finn.

Besides, just because Caleb winked at me a few times doesn't mean he's even into guys. Maybe he just flirts with all his customers to get better tips. He wouldn't be the first bartender to do that. Oh yeah, he's a bartender.

I couldn't ever be with someone who had to flirt for a living. It was bad enough being with a guitarist that always had men and women throwing themselves at him. Finn was a shameless flirt and it broke my heart every time he showed more than a friendly interest in someone else.

I guess my insecurity wasn't unfounded since he did end up cheating on me with Jack and who knows how many other people during the two years we were together. I'd heard rumors about him hooking up with fans when I wasn't around but I didn't believe it.

He was a jerk at times but he wasn't ever sleazy. At least not that I knew about.

When I lower the sheet so Caleb's back is exposed, I'm surprised to see dark marks around his hips. Not sure if my eyes are just playing tricks on me in the dim lighting, I run my thumbs from the center of his spine outward, over the marks. Caleb's sharp intake of breath confirms my suspicion.

"Are these bruises?"

When I place my thumbs at the centermost tip and wrap my hands around his hips, the marks line up perfectly. These are handprints. And there is only one way I can imagine getting handprints in that spot.

Caleb's body tenses up at my question. After a few seconds, he slowly exhales. "Uh, yeah. Sorry."

"Sorry?" I move my focus back to his spine and try to avoid the tender skin. "Why are you apologizing to me? You're the one with the marks on your back."

Now that I know what to look for, I realize the shadows around his neck aren't actually shadows. They're bruises too. He said he was sore from work but obviously that was a lie. He clearly likes rough sex if he's being manhandled like that.

"I mean, sorry I didn't mention them earlier. I think that form asked if I had any injuries and I forgot about those."

"That's okay." Caleb's body slowly relaxes as I continue to focus on his back. Before I let my imagination get away from me, I pull the sheet back over his back and expose his left foot.

His feet are baby soft and extremely ticklish. After just a few light then firm strokes across the length of his foot, he's wiggling uncomfortably on the table.

"Ticklish, I see?" I smile at his childlike nature. It almost makes me feel dirty for being so attracted to him when he's obviously so much younger than me.

"Just a little." He pants out.

I press firmly to a few pressure points then quickly move up to his calf. The moans and whimpers are back. Caleb has small but tight muscles throughout his body but his legs and calves are particularly sexy. His hair is just a baby fine dusting of blond that I find myself running my fingers over.

When I tuck the sheet under his right thigh and pull his knee out to give me better access to the full thigh, his breath hitches again. "If I do anything that makes you uncomfortable, please let me know."

"Mmm hmm." Caleb lifts his face just an inch off the pad and turns in my direction. "I can't remember ever being this comfortable. Keep going."

Well, that's encouraging. At least he doesn't think I'm a perv for trying to feel him up.

By the time I work my way up to his right thigh, I swear he's asleep. He's not making sounds anymore and he's completely pliant in my hands. I feel bad making him flip over but I want to make sure I have plenty of time on his neck and scalp before we're done.

Pulling the sheet back down over his feet, I plant my hand in the center of his back to get his attention. "Caleb?"

"Are you done already?"

"Not yet." I smile. "I'm going to lift the sheet then I'd like you to roll onto you back and scoot down so your head is flat on the table."

I reach across his body and lift the sheet from the far side so he's not exposed to me at all. Caleb starts to lift up then drops back down. "Um."

"Is everything okay?" I lower the sheet so he doesn't get cold. Does he think I'm trying to catch a peek at him?

"Well...this is embarrassing but...I'm a little...um, excited right now."

Ah. That. I don't want to smirk but I can't help myself.

"Oh, that's okay." I raise the sheet again. "It's not uncommon. Especially for a first timer. I promise not to judge you."

Caleb slowly rolls onto his back and scoots down, leaving his legs bent to help hide his erection under the thin sheet.

"You sure it's normal? I don't want to freak you out or anything."

Ignoring his bent legs, I gently lift one arm out from under the sheet and start working on his hand. "Very normal. It happens to the best of us. Of course," I peek up and see Caleb is staring intently at my face, "sometimes people come in with less than innocent intentions."

"Really?" He relaxes enough to lower his legs. There is still a slight bulge at his center but nothing embarrassing. In fact, if that's his relaxed state, he should be proud. "What do you do when that happens?"

"Explain that I don't offer those kind of services and pretty much ignore them." I interlace my fingers with Caleb's and gently tug. I can't help but notice how good his hand looks in mine. When I glance up again, he seems to be thinking the same thing with his eyes locked on our hands.

"And that's it. They don't bug you for more?"

"Don't get me wrong. I've certainly been asked to give happy endings by men and women over the years. One guy offered me a grand just for a hand job." I shake my head. "Crazy."

"And you seriously didn't do it?" Caleb has a grin on his face but he doesn't seem disgusted. Although he doesn't seem to believe me.

"God no!" I tuck his arm under the sheet and move back down to his left foot. Careful not to rub the bottom of his foot, I rotate his ankle. "There is no amount of money that could tempt me to sell myself. I guess I'm old fashioned but I believe sex should come after love. I'm nobody's whore."

Caleb's body stiffens again. His eyes are locked on the ceiling and he seems to be in pain. "I'm sorry. Did I hurt you?" I lower his leg onto the table. "I guess I'm a little sensitive about the topic so I might have been too rough."

He doesn't respond at all so I shake his foot. "Caleb? Are you okay?"

He nods but doesn't look at me.

"Did I hurt you?" I ask again. I don't see any bruising on his legs but maybe he's sore from a workout.

"Nope. Keep going." His voice is quiet like he's holding his breath.

"Okay."

I finish the massage in silence. When I turn up the lights and pat his foot, he doesn't look the same as he did when he arrived. His eyes seem rimmed in red. Damn, I knew I was too rough on his legs.

"I'll step out of the room while you get dressed. Just meet me outside when you're ready."

He nods and turns away from me, staring at the wall while I leave the room. Fuck. I was excited to maybe have a new friend and now he won't even look at me.

I'm barely able to grab a cup of water and get back to the door before Caleb pulls open the door and barrels out. Yeah, he's pissed.

"Here's some water." I try to hand it to him.

"No, thanks." He keeps walking toward the locker room. "I'm all set."

"Um, well, is there anything else you need?"

"Nope." He pushes open the locker room door and marches straight to his locker.

I know I shouldn't but I follow him in. We're still alone so I'm not likely to offend anyone. And I've already offended the one person I was eager to please. "Please tell me what I did wrong. If I hurt you, it wasn't intentional."

"You didn't do anything wrong." He lets out a deep breath then leans his forehead on the locker. "The massage was great. I feel better already."

"Oh, okay." That's a hundred eighty degree turn from the hostility he exuded just a few minutes ago. "Anytime you want to come back, just make an appointment. Until I build up a full client base, they are letting me comp a few treatments every week so you shouldn't have to pay for a while."

"I'll pay you." He finally looks at me. "And don't worry. I won't expect any special services from you."

"I know." Does he think I was trying to turn him down? I wasn't suggesting he wanted anything inappropriate from me. Shit. No wonder he's pissed. I would be too. "Caleb, I know you weren't trying to proposition me. I'm sorry if it seemed like I was turning you down. I was just oversharing, I guess. Obviously, it's not the most appropriate topic. I'm so sorry."

"Don't apologize. I get it." He opens his locker and pulls out his jeans, slipping them on under his robe. "You're not a whore."

"Okay, well, I'm sorry for what I said. I hope you do feel better."

Not sure how to make this right, I turn away and leave him to dress in peace. I've already creeped him out. Hovering while he puts on his clothes isn't going to make it better.

CHAPTER FIVE

CALEB

Fuck him and the high horse he rode in on. I know prostitution isn't exactly a respectable career choice but he couldn't even joke around about it. Who goes from peaceful massage to a soapbox about the sickos that contribute to the world's oldest profession? Self-righteous assholes, that's who.

I can't get out of here fast enough. When I try to pay, the woman reminds me this is a new client promotion and there is no charge. She hands me a small envelope to leave a gratuity in. So many petty things run through my mind as I look at the envelope. I could be an ass and leave him five bucks. But that's not cool. It's not his fault he has morals and dignity and all the other things I apparently lost years ago when I landed on the street.

In the end, I shove forty bucks in the envelope and walk out. As pissed off as I am, my anger is quickly being replaced by humiliation. I've never been as ashamed of myself as I am right now. I don't know why I think people will look beyond my source of income and see me for the person I am. I try to be kind and generous and thoughtful. But that's not enough.

I pick up litter when no one is looking. I offer to carry groceries for the women in my building who need a hand. I give cash to homeless people every chance I get because I know how easily that could have been me. Still could be.

But all the good deeds in the world can't erase the big black spot on my soul. I let strangers, or near strangers, have sex with me for money. Regardless of where that money will go or how I might be living without it, it's still disgusting and wrong and I know it.

Not able to look at anyone tonight, I thumb out a quick text to Tony.

NOT FEELING WELL. I'LL SEE YOU GUYS TOMORROW. TELL RAY NOT TO WORRY.

He quickly responds. YOU SURE YOU'RE OKAY? NEED ANYTHING?

Tony's a good guy. I've never called in sick so I can understand his concern. I wish he could bring me something to make the mortification and sadness go away.

JUST NEED SOME REST. I'LL BE GOOD TOMORROW.

As soon as I know I don't have to leave my apartment for the night, I strip out of my clothes and climb into my bed. I should shower to clear my skin of whatever oils Patton rubbed on me but despite how it ended, that was one of the best hours of my life.

The slow and deliberate care he took over every inch of my body almost brought me to tears. No one has taken care of me like that in a long time. A very long time. His fingers knew exactly where to press and glide to relieve my tense muscles. He knew when to apply a lot of pressure and when to graze my skin with a gentle touch.

Every movement was planned to make me feel good. Cared for. Like I deserved care and attention. He gave me both and didn't ask for anything in return. I didn't even have to pay for it.

Fuck! I'm an asshole. He didn't do anything wrong and I completely blew up. He's just a good guy trying to help out a stranger and I acted like he kicked my puppy.

I'm sure I'll never see him again but if I do, I'll apologize with some excuse about why I turned into super dick. Although I hope I don't see him again because the chances of him coming back into Ray's and not learning about my other job are pretty slim. And for the first time ever, I really don't want him to know the truth. I'm too ashamed of myself to be honest with such a good guy.

~**~

I still feel a little depressed when I walk into Ray's on Friday night. I'm working the bar so at least I don't have to put out for anyone. I probably couldn't get it up if I tried. Well, I could if I imagined a certain surfer boy rubbing his soft hands across my naked skin...

"Feeling better, kid?" I feel Tony's hand on my shoulder before I hear his words.

My smile is small but genuine when I look up at the giant beside me. At six four, no one messes with Tony. He's a three hundred pound teddy bear to his friends but a rabid pit bull to his enemies. I'm grateful to count him as a friend for more than a few reasons.

"Much. Thanks, man." I walk to the break room with Tony and slip off my coat. "Did I miss anything last night?"

"Not much." An evil smile spreads across his face. "But that fucker you told me about came by."

"Ron?" Shit. I totally forgot about him. I guess it's a good thing I wasn't in and didn't have to confront him personally. I don't like confrontations so it's always hard for me to say no to people. Especially if they're being nice. "What happened?"

"He waited around for a while before finally asking where you were." Tony chuckled quietly which made me nervous. He could do serious damage if he wanted to.

"And?" I wave my hand forward in a gesture for him to keep talking. "Then what?"

"I explained that you've decided to limit your appointments and he didn't make the cut."

Tony just stares at me with a frightening smirk on his face.

"So he just left?" I find that hard to believe.

"Nope." He laughs louder now. "He needed a little incentive."

My jaw drops and I feel a little faint. "Is he okay?" I whisper.

"No permanent damage but I don't think he'll be back."

"Damn." I exhale slowly. "Well, thanks for that. I don't know if I could have gotten rid of him on my own."

Tony pulls me into a side hug. "Anytime, kid. You know that."

I turn into his chest and wrap both arms around him, catching him off guard. "I know, Tony. You're the best."

It takes a minute before I feel both of his arms close around me. "Yeah, of course." He pats my back awkwardly then pulls away, looking me in the eye. "You sure you're okay? You're not dying or anything, are you?"

I smile and swipe at the tear that has fallen to my cheek. "I'm fine. Just still a little out of it and it feels good to know you've got my back."

I nod several times, reassuring myself and Tony that I'm okay.

"Always, kid." He squeezes my shoulder then backs away. "I better get back out there before all hell breaks loose."

By the time I take my place behind the bar, I'm in a better mood. I have friends that love me despite my choices. They don't judge me for what I do. They judge me for who I am. And, whether a guy like Patton Oliver would ever agree or not, I'm a good person that shouldn't have to hide his lifestyle.

I've never been in the closet about my sexuality and I don't intend to hide in one about my profession. If anyone has a problem with it, they can kiss my ass.

Dylan and Spencer come in at ten and take a seat at the bar. "Hey, beautiful." Dylan looks like a runway model and his boyfriend is one of those geeky chic computer guys. They're a cute couple.

"Hey, Dyl." I reach across the bar to bump his fist and then his partner's. "Spence. What brings you guys out tonight?"

Spencer just moved into Dylan's house from California and they've been inseparable. It's actually sweet to watch them fawn all over each other. Sweet and sickening. But mostly sweet.

"Just wanted a drink." Dylan says. "Can we get a couple Crown and Cokes?"

"Of course." I nod and reach for the Crown. "Haven't seen you guys since your New Year's party."

Spencer's face turns a bright red. "Well, we've been cooped up in the apartment for a few weeks. Decided it was time to start socializing again."

When I slide the glasses across the table, I can't help but envy the easy way they are with each other. Their loving gazes are deep and unabashed. They get lost in each other and I seem to not exist anymore. Giving them their privacy, I step away and walk to the other end of the bar to refill a few drinks.

Dylan walks behind my customer and nods to me. "Hey, Caleb. Stop by when you have a few minutes. We want to ask you about something."

I quirk an eyebrow in question but nod and get back to the customer in front of me. For the next twenty minutes, I can't stop wondering what Dylan might want from me.

As soon as Vinnie gets back from his break, I tell him I'm taking mine and head over to the corner booth Spencer and Dylan are huddled in.

"Hey, guys." I slide into the booth and lean back. "What's up?"

Dylan pulls out of Spencer's arms and sits forward. "Well, I was wondering how things are going for you."

What? He's never shown more than a passing interest in me before so I'm immediately on alert. Also sitting forward, I glance at Spencer before responding.

"Um, I'm fine. Why do you ask?"

"You know I manage the *personal entertainment* side of Paddles as well as the arcade business, right?"

Steve has given me the short story of how he met Dylan when the crime family he worked for was shaken up. Now Dylan runs the stable of rent boys as well as the public arcade they use to launder the money.

I shrug, feeling uncomfortable with where the conversation is going. "Yeah, I guess I've heard something about that."

Dylan slides a card across the table. "I just wanted to let you know that if you ever wanted a job with higher level clients, I'd love to have you."

"You're offering me a job?" It's starting to make a lot more sense. Instead of being a bar fly whore, I'd be a high dollar escort. Look, Ma, a promotion.

"Steve speaks highly of you and if you're as smart as he says you are, I'm sure we can find a place for you in the organization." He lifts his glass and swirls the remaining liquid around before finishing it. "Room and board is included and you keep all your tips."

"I'd live there?" Not having to waste money on rent would be nice. "At the arcade?"

"We own the building. A few floors are private residences and the rest are for business use, but yes, you could live on site and eat in the common areas so your expense will be minimal."

Spencer finally leans forward and grins. "You'd even have benefits."

"Seriously?" How is that even possible?

"What do you think?" Dylan has a gorgeous smile that tells me he presumes to know my answer.

A week ago I might have jumped at the opportunity. But now I'm not sure. I don't actually want to be a hooker, high class or otherwise, for much longer. It probably isn't fair to accept the job and move in...only to leave as soon as I graduate. I look Dylan straight in the eyes and smile. "Thank you, Dylan. I appreciate the offer but I'll need to think about it."

"Of course. Take your time." He seems taken aback by my lack of acceptance but extends his hand to me. "The offer will remain open so if you decide to take me up on it, just let me know."

"Thanks." I nod curtly then stand. "I better get back to work."

They both say goodbye and I quickly rejoin Vinnie. The number of people hovering around the bar seems to have doubled in the past ten minutes so I jump back into the fray.

For the rest of the night, I focus on pouring booze and nothing else. No chocolate brown eyes behind sun bleached hair. No rent free apartments and fat tips. And definitely no life away from hustling. I can't begin to think about that for a few more years.

Chapter Six

Patton

I don't know what I did to piss off Caleb but I can't stop thinking about him. I've run our last conversation through my head a thousand times and nothing makes sense. If he did think I was turning him down, I could see him being embarrassed or disgusted but I don't understand the anger.

I want to give him space and a few days to calm down but after two days of stewing in my frustration, I need to go talk to him. He left his number on the new client form but I don't want to stoop to the point of stealing it. If he wants me to have his personal number, he'll give it to me. Until then, I have to reach him in the only way I know how. At his place of employment.

Ray's is packed tonight. It's just after eight on Saturday but there's a convention in town so everything is busy. I walk to the bar to find Caleb but he's not working. Slipping onto the first stool that opens up, I order a Tanq and Tonic from the cute redhead. He looks to be a few years older than me but has a sexy Ed Sheeran thing going on.

I slip him the cash and ask if Caleb is working tonight. He stills for a second and looks me over. After a moment of contemplation, he juts his chin out toward the center of the bar. "He's at a table over there."

Spinning around with my beer in hand, I'm about to stand when I see Caleb sitting at a table with an older man. The man has his hand on the back of Caleb's neck and leans in to whisper in his ear.

The sexy smile Caleb flashes is like a kick in the gut. If he has a boyfriend, that might explain why he was so offended by my accusations.

I feel even worse about my behavior. That conversation was completely inappropriate and unprofessional. I'm lucky he hasn't called the owner of Hydrate to complain. That would just be my luck. Move from Colorado to Oregon to start a new life and get fired after two months.

I have to apologize. I look up again and see Caleb pulling the man toward the employees only hallway. Taking my drink, I walk to one of the few empty tables in the place and sit my ass down. I can wait a few minutes to see if they come back and then I'll apologize to Caleb.

My table is in a far corner, closer to the pool tables but with a clear view of the door they disappeared through. With one eye focused on the door, I watch the guys playing pool.

There are two tables and both groups have a mix of couples of making out and others that are just focused on the game. That used to be my life.

When Finn and I started our cover band, it was just for fun. I like to sing and he played guitar so we'd sit around my apartment and jam every night. When one of his cousins needed a band for a wedding, we found a few other friends and *Oiled Up* was formed.

Within a few months, we'd booked several weddings and office parties and played dive bars on the weekends. There wasn't much money involved but it was fun and a great way to spend time with the man I loved. The man I thought loved me. That all fell apart when I started working more evening shifts at my old spa and the rumors of Finn and Jack started. I didn't believe them at first but when I came home early one day and found them in bed, all bets were off.

I kicked Finn out of my apartment and out of my life. For the most part. That was six months ago and I'm trying to be the bigger person by not holding a grudge. Obviously, he and I weren't meant to be. I'm honestly glad he cheated sooner rather than later.

If we had gotten married or even engaged, I would have been more devastated. I was sick for a week but I think I knew deep down that things weren't going to last. There was always something about Finn that I couldn't quite trust. Something he held back. And the way he joked about me giving happy endings at work for extra tips has made me particularly sensitive to the subject.

Finn wasn't the one but I believe there is one out there for me. For a few days, I toyed with the idea of Caleb being the one. Obviously, I'm a day late and a dollar short because he's already taken.

Movement from the employee door catches my eye. The man Caleb walked out with is coming back. He's tucking in the front of his shirt and zipping up his jeans. Holy shit. They just went back there for a quickie. I glance at my watch. Twenty-five minutes. I guess that's not too quick. Towards the end, I was lucky to get ten minutes with Finn so twenty-five is basically a slowie.

Since when does one drink make me loopy? Oh yeah, I haven't eaten anything today. I stand to meet Caleb on his way out but he's not behind the guy. The man rejoins a group of guys at a table by the front and doesn't offer a backward glance toward the employee door.

Maybe he went out the back? Just as the thought enters my head, Caleb walks out. He's a mouthwatering mix of sexy and innocent. His bright blue eyes set off the blond streaks in his hair that I want to run my fingers through. Every part of his body is smooth and firm. Even his hair is like a soft layer of down on his perfect body. Standing like an idiot, I put my empty glass on the table and take one step forward just as another guy walks into Caleb's embrace. Like the first man, he leans into Caleb's neck and seems to be whispering to him. The smile on his face is just as sensual as he offered the first man but when Caleb's gaze locks onto mine, his smile drops.

His face takes on a crimson tone which could either be from anger or shame. From this distance, I can't tell. I take another step toward him and he just shakes his head once. It's subtle but I don't miss it.

I take a step back as if he's slapped me in the face. That's when he looks toward his new friend and smiles. He turns back to the employee door and drags his friend through it.

What the fuck is going on? I have to sit down again before I collapse. The puzzle pieces of my interactions with Caleb are starting to fit together.

The bruises on his neck and hips. His instant reaction to my diatribe about how disgusting prostitution is. The first guy coming out and zipping up his pants. Oh my god.

I have to get out of here. Standing up with a little too much force, the wooden chair I'm on flies back and bangs against the ground loudly. I don't bother to pick it up. I think I might be sick as I run for the door.

I hear wannabe Ed Sheeran asking if I'm okay but I don't look back. I can't believe how this night has gone. I walked in with a plan to apologize and maybe ask Caleb out to dinner. He's the kind of guy I thought I could hang out with. Maybe date. Maybe more. But now that's all out the fucking window.

CHAPTER SEVEN

CALEB

I should have known the night wouldn't be as smooth as it started. After a few easy tricks, seeing Kevin walk up to me was like a bonus. He's a bottom and actually likes me to enjoy it. I haven't seen him in a while but I always have fun with him.

His stubbly cheek brushes mine as he leans into my neck and places a kiss just below my ear. "Hey, sexy."

My neck is almost as ticklish as my feet so I giggle and wrap my arms around him. "Kev, hey. It's great to see you."

With a light drag of his tongue across my earlobe, I'm putty in his hands. "You have time for me?"

"Always." I exhale some of the tension I've been holding since my disastrous massage and look up. Patton is standing on the other side of the room, staring at me. My stomach drops as his eyes bore into me.

Why the fuck is he here? Didn't I make it clear I have nothing to say to him? He takes a step toward me and my head moves just half an inch to the right then back. He's confused about my reaction but he steps back.

I don't have time to deal with him tonight. I've got bills to pay and dicks to suck. Fuck, Patton.

I turn and pull Kevin back through the door I just emerged from. The revolving door of casual sex for hire that I've bet my financial future on. Just a few more years and I'll be done. I can put this all behind me and start living my life.

Until then, I have a sweet man in my arms that is looking for some attention. He's come to the right place. As soon as the door to the office is closed behind us, Kevin takes my mouth in his. I don't like kissing but it's part of the job.

By the time we make it to the couch, we're both breathless. I run my hands underneath his shirt. "What do you have in mind, big guy?"

Kevin slides his hand over the front of my jeans, tracing my cock with his finger. "I want you to fuck me."

"I think I can make that happen." We quickly strip and get to it. I feel guilty for it but I keep seeing flashes of Patton's face as I pound into Kevin. His eyes are closed too so who knows who he's picturing above him. We're both getting what we need at the moment.

By the time we're both spent, Patton is out of my mind. For a few minutes at least.

~**~

"Cay." Vinnie snaps my ass with a towel as soon as I get behind the bar.

"Yeah." I pour a cup of water for myself and lean against the back wall.

"Some guy was looking for you earlier."

My eyes dart over to him without moving my head. "Surfer boy?"

"That's the one." He gets right up in my face and smirks. "He's smokin hot."

"You can tell him that if he ever comes back." I take the last gulp of water then toss the plastic cup in the trash. "Because he won't be back to see me."

"No?" Vinnie looks as disappointed as I feel at the reality of it. "You sure? He seemed anxious to see you."

I bark out a laugh. "Yeah, I'm sure. He's not exactly the type to share...if you know what I mean."

"Oh, that?" Vinnie nods his head to gesture upstairs. "Yeah, well, I can see how that would be hard to accept."

"Yup." I glance at the bottle of Crown just a few inches from my hand. If anyone deserves to get drunk on a Saturday night, I think it's me. But my stomach is still in a knot from seeing Patton. Just the thought of liquor makes me feel nauseous. "I'm basically untouchable at this point in my life."

"That," Vinnie pulls me into his arms and squeezes hard, "is not true. You're absolutely touchable and he's an idiot if he can't deal with your job for a while longer until you move on."

"Yeah." Maybe moving on is exactly what I need to do. What the hell am I waiting for anyway? Ray's been like a father to me and I could never repay him for all he's done but I also know I'm putting him and his bar at risk every time I take the walk of shame upstairs. Any one of those guys could be a cop looking to teach bar owners a lesson. "That might actually be sooner rather than later."

Vinnie pulls back and notices a customer. "Walk with me."

I follow as he heads to the far end of the bar.

"What the hell are you talking about?"

"You know Dylan? Steve's friend?"

"Yeah." Everyone remembers when Steve and Joey started bringing around the gorgeous body guard that took over Paddles. He was everybody's favorite friend for a few weeks there. But when it became apparent he was stuck on his California dot com geek, we all gave up hope.

Honestly, I'm a little surprised it took him so long to approach me. The way he watched me the first few nights he came in, I expected a job offer, or even just a request for a demonstration, months ago.

"He offered me a job in his stable. It would include an apartment in the Paddles building and benefits and shit. I'm thinking about taking it." I blow out a deep breath and wait for his response.

"Seriously?" He looks around the room, resting his eyes on Ray and Tony. "You talk to Ray yet?"

"No." I lean my head back and cover my eyes with my laced fingers. "I'm still not sure what to do."

"You know we'll miss you around here every day but if you have an opportunity to better your life...you should take it."

"I think I might." I give Vinnie a pat on the back and head out. "I'll be in tomorrow."

"Be good, man."

CHAPTER EIGHT

PATTON

For the past two weeks, I've been replaying that night at Ray's in my mind over and over. I want to remember it different than how it played out. Did the other guy look like he could be a brother? Maybe a coworker? Any possibility the first guy was his dad. If either of those guys were relatives then Caleb is even kinkier than I thought.

Sometimes a duck is just a duck and a prostitute is just a prostitute. I hate that Caleb sells his body but I'm starting to hate myself even more for not being able to at least talk to him. Hear his story.

Maybe be his friend. He's still the sweet bartender that I watched for hours that first night. I'm not exactly overflowing with friends so if I can get past my own prejudices, maybe we can hang out sometime.

I've talked myself out of going to Ray's every night since then but I'm not sure what I can say that will not be insulting or judgmental so I haven't done it. Maybe tonight?

Just as I'm walking up the stairs to my apartment, the front door below me opens. Heather has her phone to her ear as she waves me down. "Patton, thank god you're home."

I back track the two steps I've taken and head to her. "Everything okay?" I peek into her apartment and see Charlie Ann playing with some books on the floor.

"Yeah, Patton is here. When can you get here?"

I look to her but her palm is out as she listens to her phone. She's stepping into shoes and pulling a scarf around her neck. She appears to be leaving but her one-year-old daughter doesn't look like she's going anywhere.

"Okay, just hurry." Heather clicks off her phone and drops it into her bag before finally turning back to me. "I need a favor."

I look at her coat and her kid then smirk. "Let me guess. Your babysitter cancelled?"

"I wish." She pulls a bag of Goldfish out of her pantry and fills a sippy cup with water then lines them both up on the counter. "The sprinklers went off at the boutique and I need to go move merchandise before it's all destroyed."

She runs to Charlie and places a quick kiss on her head. "Dylan can't get here for about an hour. Can you please, please, please stay with her until he arrives? She's already eaten and will probably just pass out on the floor. You can leave her there until Dylan arrives or put her in bed. Whatever."

"Yeah, she's the best company I've had in months." Heather starts digging through her purse, pulling stuff out. I pull her keys out from under the Goldfish bag and hand them to her. "We'll be fine."

"Oh, you're the best." She jumps into my arms and kisses my cheek. "I still think Dylan should have chosen you but Spencer is pretty cool."

I nod and lock the door after she runs through it. Well, looks like I've finally got a date.

Charlie is an easy baby. She doesn't even look up when her mom walks out the door. I drop onto the sofa behind her and grab the remote. A cartoon about a princess named Sofia comes on and Charlie jumps off the floor and runs to the TV. Spreading her palms on the flat screen, she starts bouncing on her cubby legs, singing along in her baby babble. It's the cutest thing I've ever seen.

I'm tempted to make a video for Heather but she probably sees this every day so I just sit back and watch.

After twenty minutes of singing along, Charlie gets tired and finally looks back at me. At first, she's a little shocked as if she didn't know I was there. But I've spent enough time with her and her momma that she just climbs onto me and sprawls across my chest.

Her little body is warm and smells like baby shampoo. I take a whiff and run my fingers through her hair as she lets out a deep breath. Her blonde strands are fine and silky, just like Caleb's. I really need to stop thinking about that kid. Closing my eyes, I imagine what it would be like to have this. A baby. A family. I thought that was part of my future with Finn. Now it seems like a distant dream meant for someone else entirely.

I don't know how long I was asleep but the TV noise drowned out the sound of Dylan coming in. I didn't wake up until I heard a camera click above me.

When my eyes shoot open, Dylan's sculpted face is staring me down from above his phone. "Asleep on the job, I see."

Charlie is still spread across my chest, sleeping soundly. Holding her against me, I carefully sit up then carry her to her crib.

When I walk back out, Dylan hands me a beer. "Figured you might need this."

"Thanks." I grab it and take a drink. "She was no trouble. Obviously."

"Yeah." Dylan shakes his head and looks toward his niece's bedroom. "She didn't get that from her mother."

I chuckle. Heather is a bit of a handful. But I adore her. She's one of the few people I can call a friend in the entire state.

"Hey, a friend is having a birthday thing over at Ray's on Friday. You should come."

I freeze for a moment then look at Dylan. "Ray's? You go there a lot?"

"Not too often but Spence and I are trying to socialize a bit more often." He takes a drink and raises an eyebrow to me. "You been there?"

"Just a few times." I clear my throat. "Do you know a guy named Caleb?"

A slow smirk crosses Dylan's face. "I do know Caleb."

"Do you think he'll be there?"

"I know he's invited but I'm not sure if he'll be working or not."

"Oh, cool." I pick at the hem of my shirt. Unable to look him in the eye.

"So, how do you know Caleb?" I can feel Dylan watching me like a hawk. I chance a quick glance his way.

"I met him a few times at Ray's."

"Oh..."

"Oh?" *Oh*. He thinks... "No, not like that. I was his customer."

Dylan laughs. "I'm sure you were."

I can feel my face burning. "No, not that kind. At the bar. He served me drinks."

Dylan laughs. "Chill, man."

I sound like a damn liar. I've got to get out of here before I make an even bigger fool of myself. "Yeah, well, I better get going. Tell Heather to call me if she needs anything."

"Thanks for watching Charlie." Dylan opens the front door. "I'll see you Friday."

When I finally get settled into my apartment, the quiet is claustrophobic. I've never liked being single and the weight of my loneliness is becoming oppressive. I love my job and my clientele is starting to build up so I know I'll have a full schedule within the next few months. But that's not enough. I want someone to come home to. Someone waiting to take care of me. Someone just for me. Unfortunately, Caleb isn't that person. He's available to the world...for the right price.

CHAPTER NINE

CALEB

With mixed feelings, I call Dylan and accept his job offer. He sounds happy to have me on board. There is an empty apartment on the fifth floor so after classes, I load up my old Honda Accord and begin moving into the Paddles building.

The first floor is a huge arcade for kids and adults. It's like your typical Dave and Busters without the full restaurant. Just a snack bar to keep people hydrated and spending money.

I park in the underground garage and take the elevator up to Dylan's penthouse apartment.

"You must be Caleb! Come in, come in!" A very flamboyant man with hot pink hair and a matching silk kimono opens the door and motions me in. "You're even yummier than Dylan said you'd be."

"Um, thank you." I drag my suitcase and a duffle bag in with me.

He pulls me into a hug and kisses both cheeks. "I'm Georgie, but you probably already know that."

"Good to meet you, Georgie." I don't want to admit that I have no idea who he is. But since he knows me, I can roll with it. "Is Dylan here?"

"He just got called downstairs." Georgie walks to the kitchen. "Can I get you something to drink before I take you on the grand tour?"

"No, thanks." This apartment is amazing. The whole back wall is a window to the city. It must be breathtaking at night. If this is where Dylan lives, business must be doing well.

"Fine." Let me just get dressed and I'll be right back.

Georgie emerges a few minutes later in shiny leggings and a tight yellow t-shirt.

We take the elevator to the fifth floor and Georgie hands me a key. "You get one of the newly remodeled apartments. 612. Home sweet home."

"I do?" I grab the key and stick it in the deadbolt. "That's cool."

"Yeah, there was some water damage last year and this unit was gutted. It's way nicer than most of the standard places."

As I walk inside, I have to catch my breath. It looks like a model house for some architectural magazine. The kitchen has stainless steel appliances and black stone counters. The living room has the same wall of windows as the penthouse but it's only a quarter of the size.

"It's fully furnished?" I look to Georgie. This means I can dump the plaid green couch I bought at Salvation Army for twenty bucks.

"Yup." He runs his hand across the back of the black leather sofa. "They call this Bugatti Leather. Same as in a Bugatti."

"Damn." I'm afraid to touch it. "Maybe I can put a sheet over it to keep it clean."

Georgie's laugh quickly turns into a scowl. "Uh, no. You will not cover up such beauty. Topher let some designer have a field day in the new apartments. Same designer he used for our place."

"You live in the penthouse too? With Dylan?"

"Yeah." He walks toward a pair of dark wood French doors. "Spencer pretty much lives there too so maybe I'll take one of the other apartments. Haven't decided yet."

When Georgie pushes open the doors, I have to pinch myself. "Seriously? This is my room?"

"It is!" Georgie skips to the bed then hops in the air and lands in the middle of it on his ass. "And it's so comfy. You'll never want to leave it."

"You've been in this bed before?" I have to smile. He's a character, that's for sure.

"This used to be Adam's place. He wasn't here for very long but he was delish."

I walk in and run my hand across the velvety bed cover. It's softer than anything I've ever felt before. If Georgie wasn't here, I'd roll around on it too. "Who's Adam?"

"One of the guys that used to work here. When Topher left, he decided to move on too."

I nod slowly. Topher had most of his boys on contracts they couldn't break. No one left unless he wanted them gone. And if he wanted you gone, you were almost never found.

Once he was *eliminated* from the family business, the guys were all given the option of leaving. I guess Adam was one who took it.

"Okay, what else?" Georgie rolls onto his belly and rests his chin in his hands while swinging his calves in the air. "The house cleaners come every Monday and Thursday. We are discouraged from bringing clients to our own apartments, for safety reasons, but let Josh or Marco know if you have special requests."

At the new names, I hold up my hand. "Who are Josh and Marco?"

"They run security. They have cameras in all the halls and stairwells and keep track of who is where. Most of the time, you'll meet clients in the suites on the third and fourth floors. I'll show you those later."

He flips over onto his back then leans up on one elbow. "Dr. Jenner can come on Thursday at lunch but if you want to go to his office sooner for testing, his card is on the dresser."

"Testing?" Dylan didn't mention it but I guess that makes sense.

"Yeah. They're really strict about it. Every two months or no clients." Georgie crawls to the edge and pulls out the night stand drawer. "Both drawers are stocked with lube and condoms in each unit. Same with the end tables in the living rooms. It's like a sex ed teacher's wet dream around here."

I have to laugh. "Well, that'll save me some money, I guess."

Georgie looks serious for the first time since I met him. "So what's your story? How did you end up here?"

I take a deep breath. "It's not the most exciting story. My parents knew I was gay from the time I was in middle school. I didn't do anything to flaunt it but I couldn't completely hide it either. As soon as I was eighteen, they gave me the money they had saved for college and sent me on my way. I drove for two days. Ended up here and have been working my way through school ever since."

"Hmm." He sits up and crosses his legs on the bed. "Well, that's not so bad. At least you had some cash. Most of us didn't get more than a firm kick in the ass on our way out."

I cock my head and look at Georgie with new eyes. As much as I like to feel sorry for myself, I know I've been lucky. Life could have been much worse for me. "What about you? How did you wind up in the penthouse?"

"Welp," he claps his hands dramatically, "I was a dancer at Manhandled since I was sixteen. Topher found me there and asked me to be one of his private dancers about two years ago. The rest is history."

"So you like it here?" I know the answer but it seems prudent to ask before I move everything in. If there is a dark side, I'd like to know it before I'm fully committed.

"Love." He stands up and walks to the open window. "Waking up to this view every morning and getting paid serious cash to please beautiful men every night. How could I not?"

"I suppose." And that's my biggest fear. I'll love this lifestyle so much that I'll never want to leave. "Does that mean you're a lifer?"

"God, no." Georgie visibly shudders at the thought. "I'm saving up to start a clothing line. I've been taking some online fashion design classes and will probably move to New York at some point. Unless I find a sugar daddy to keep me here."

"So you'd give up all this for a man?" I'm not sure why I'm so surprised but I didn't expect that from him.

"Of course." Georgie walks back and places his hand on my shoulder. "This is a job like any other. Just a means to an end. We all have a different end point...but for most of us, it's when we decide to settle down with someone worth more than a fancy view."

CHAPTER TEN

PATTON

I don't want to go to this party but I've got nothing better to do and I need to apologize to Caleb for the multiple times I treated him like an ass. The more I think about it, the more I know the problem is mine and not his.

He's a smart kid that has chosen a path in life that I wouldn't have chosen but that doesn't make him a bad person. He doesn't appear to be strung out or hurting anyone so who am I to judge?

Honestly, it's not that different from what I do for a living. The pleasure I give to people isn't quite as carnal but it's still physical. Is there really a difference?

I get to Ray's just after nine. There's a decent crowd but only a few faces I recognize. Caleb's isn't one of them. I head to the bar and order my usual from the cute redhead.

"So, what's your name, anyway?" I ask as I lay a ten on the counter.

"Vinnie." He slides my drink to me and shakes his head at the money. "Drinks are on Spencer tonight."

"Vinnie?" I squint my eyes and tilt my head to the side. "You don't look like a Vinnie."

"You don't know any ginger Vinnies?" He furrows his eyebrows before laughing at his own joke. "It's short for Gavin."

"Ah, that suits you." I take a drink, savoring the tangy lime.

"And do you go by anything other than surfer boy?"

I almost choke at his question. "Surfer boy? Who calls me that?"

"Caleb?" His chin is down and he peeks up from under long lashes. "Me."

"Caleb does?" He's been talking about me? I can feel a smile forming on my face. That must have been before I made a complete jackass out of myself. "Actually, I'm Patton."

"Patton?" Now Vinnie's inspecting me. "You don't look like a Patton. A Chad or Trey, maybe. Not a Patton."

"You've never met a surfer boy named Patton?" I finish my drink and let him pour me a refill. "Supposedly, I'm related to the general in some way. Who knows if it's true but my mom liked the name."

In fact, my name was her only link to the family that disowned her. After falling in with the wrong crowd in high school, she got hooked on crack and had to sell herself to support her habit. Thanks to a sympathetic but enabling aunt, we were never homeless but I vowed early on to never give control of my mind or body to anyone or anything.

And that's really the reason I hate what Caleb is doing. Speaking of... "So, is Caleb working tonight?"

Vinnie is filling glasses with champagne when his whole body stills. He doesn't look at me until after he hands them off to the server. When he finally walks to me, he's wearing a sad expression. "He doesn't work here anymore. He quit."

"He did?" I look around the room as if Vinnie is mistaken. Caleb isn't at the table he was at last time I saw him and I don't see him among the guests. "Since when?"

"Sunday was his last day." Vinnie drops a glass hard on the counter. The noise grabs my attention. When I look up, his eyes are boring into mine. "He mentioned something about being ready to move on to the next stage in his life."

The next stage? What the hell does that mean? I couldn't have anything to do with his decision to quit, right? But what if I am? What if he is interested in me? Maybe not even sexually but if I helped him realize he deserves a better life than that of a sex worker, that would be awesome.

"That's great!" My level of enthusiasm is probably inappropriate for someone I've only met a few times but Vinnie just shakes his head and smiles.

"Yeah, it sounds like a pretty good gig. We'll miss him around here but it's a good move."

I nod and pull out my phone. "So what's he doing now? Do you have a number for him?"

Vinnie looks around the room then points over my shoulder. "He's working for Dylan Abraham. That guy in the blue shirt over there."

"Dylan?" I turn and stand, leaving my drink on the counter. "Doesn't Dylan work in an arcade?"

"Something like that." Vinnie nods to a customer waiting on the other side of the bar. "You should go talk to him. He might know how to reach Caleb."

As soon as Dylan notices me approaching, he pulls a tall guy in glasses in my direction.

"Patton, you made it." He gives me a quick hug. "I'd like you to meet my boyfriend, Spencer."

The taller guy extends his hand. "Good to meet you."

"Yeah, you too. Thanks for the drinks."

"Of course. I hope you're enjoying yourself." Spencer curls his hand around Dylan's bicep. I don't blame him. Dylan is built like a body builder.

"Yeah, it's a great party." I turn back to Dylan as if I just thought of something. "Hey, do you know if Caleb is coming tonight?"

Dylan smirks and hip checks Spencer with an arched eyebrow. "I hope so. He said he'd try to make it but I haven't seen him yet."

I take the opening while I've got it. "I heard Caleb is working for you now."

Dylan nods over the rim of his drink, keeping his eyes trained on me.

"You run an arcade, right?" I wish he'd just give me the answers without making me drag each one out of him.

"I do." That's all he gives me. I stick my hands in my pockets and rock on my heels.

"Cool." I take another look around, hoping to find something to talk about. "Is your sister coming?"

"Nah. Charlie is teething so she's too cranky for a sitter."

Great. Now Dylan's officially the only person I actually know in this place. "Okay, well, I guess I'll grab another drink."

Dylan nods then drags Spencer toward the pool tables. Not sure what else to do, I perch in a corner booth and pull out my phone. I've got three missed calls from Finn.

To avoid a fourth, I decide to text him back.

TALKED TO YOUR NEW BOSS AND LIED MY ASS OFF. GOOD LUCK.

My phone rings about thirty seconds after I hit send. Fuck. I so don't want to talk right now. But I'm a people pleaser so here we go.

"Hey, Finn. Did you see my text?"

"Yeah, thanks. I think I'm getting an offer." I can hardly hear him over the music in the background. He must be at a club. "But that's not why I was calling."

"Oh. What's up?" What I really mean is, now what do you need from me.

"You remember Dave? I used to work with him?"

"Yeah, I think so." In the two years we were together, Finn had five jobs so I'm not positive I remember Dave but it's not worth getting into a conversation over. "What about him?"

"He's getting married and his bachelor party is out your way."

"Okay." I so don't like where this is heading.

"So I'm going to be there next weekend. I can stay at your place, right?"

"Oh." Is he serious? "Well, my apartment is kinda small. I'm not sure you'll be comfortable."

"Don't worry about me. You know I can sleep anywhere."

I do know that. Anywhere and with anyone. "Isn't everyone staying together?"

"Yeah, at some fancy ass hotel. I don't want to waste money on a hotel when I can just crash with you. That way I don't have to pay for food either."

"Um." Just say no, asshole! "I guess that's okay."

"I knew you'd be cool with it."

"Is Jack coming too?" I'll have to stay at a hotel if they're both in my apartment. I don't think I can handle watching them, or god forbid, hearing them.

"Jack?" He laughs. "No way. He's old news. I'm a free agent so you might get lucky."

Shoot me now. Twice.

Chapter Eleven

Caleb

I don't know what I was so worried about. Working at Paddles is like living at the Four Seasons of brothels. The clients are all prescreened so I don't have to worry about losers. They pay in advance when they make a reservation so I don't have to deal with money other than their tips. And as soon as they leave, I get a call from security to make sure I'm okay before the john has even left the building.

The shame and self-loathing I felt just a week ago is completely gone. And if that isn't enough, I've made more money in the first days on the job than I did in most months at Ray's.

I can almost fool myself into thinking life is good. Great even. It would be if I could get Patton out of my head. But he's always there. When I sleep. When I shower. When I have a drink. Even my new boss knows him.

Dylan shocked the hell out of me when he asked me about a guy named Patton. I almost fell down the stairs we were taking to the gym.

My face must have given away something because since then, Dylan has been bugging me to go to Matty's party tonight. I'm dressed and strongly considering it but I just don't think I can handle another look of disgust on Patton's face.

The last time I saw him, it was obvious he figured out what I was doing. He wanted to say something to me, probably tell me off, but I managed to avoid that conflict, as usual. I just shook my head and sent him on his way. If I see him tonight, he might not be so complacent. He might finally tell me what he really thinks of me and I just don't think I can take it.

Besides, a scene in the middle of Ray's wouldn't be fair to Matty or to Ray. No, I'm definitely not going. I toss my keys back onto the counter and head to bed. This is only the second night I've had free in my new apartment since I fully moved in and watching movies in bed sounds better than rejection and humiliation in front of all my friends.

I've been staring at my computer screen for an hour and the numbers keep saying the same thing. Based on the tips I've already banked, I could have enough money to pay for two years at Portland State in cash before I even get my associate's degree this May. One year after that and I can quit for good and focus on starting my own business.

I'm running the numbers in a budgeting model for the hundredth time when I hear pounding on my front door. I toss my laptop onto the bed and jump up but when I hear Georgie's high pitched, "Yoo hoo, Cay Cay," I know it's nothing serious.

When I open the door, I have to laugh. Georgie is wearing a women's bikini with some kind of floral cover up that was probably popular with elderly women in the seventies. I don't know where he comes up with this stuff.

"Hi, Georgie." I open the door wide enough for him to saunter through. Yes, he saunters.

"I have a proposition for you." He sits back on my sofa and crosses his ankles on top of my coffee table. Thank god he isn't sitting with spread legs because that thong isn't holding much back.

"I can't wait to hear it." My sarcasm earns me a swat on the thigh. Then his hand circles back and massages my muscle for a few seconds. "Oh, you mean you're propositioning me?"

"No, silly. This is business." He lets his hand slide up my thigh to cup my crotch before he moves it back down. "That would be pure pleasure."

I roll my eyes. He's the epitome of drama queen. Everything he says and does is with a strong reaction in mind. Georgie loves to shock people and make them uncomfortable. He just doesn't get that from me...most of the time.

"So this business of which you speak..."

"Well, we've got a bachelor party coming in on Saturday and they've requested four entertainers. Together." He says the last word slowly to emphasize his meaning. "And there's a thousand dollar bonus if you do it."

I feel my jaw drop as I take in his words. A thousand dollar bonus for one night would be huge. And it's not like I haven't done groups before. "How long is the party?"

"They are only asking for two hours with us. Midnight to two AM." He has an adorable smile when he's excited that makes it hard to say no to.

"Who would we be working with?" I ask.

"Does it matter?" He cocks an eyebrow and studies me for a moment. "You got preferences?"

Do I? I've met most of the guys and they're all good looking. No one I'd have a problem hooking up with. "No, I guess not."

"So you'll do it?" His hands are poised to clap and his feet swing to the floor, ready to tap out his happy dance.

"Yeah, I guess so." Even though I know it's coming, I still tense for a second when Georgie hops in my lap.

"Yay, yay, yay!" He gives me a sloppy, wet kiss on the cheek. "We're gonna have so much fun."

"Are you always this excited for groups?"

"When there's fresh blood on the menu, fuck yeah I am."

Oh god. Does he mean me or the clients? I don't even want to ask.

~**~

"Are you sure I look okay?" I don't know what possessed me to let Georgie dress me for this party but he seems to know what he's doing.

"You're a vision." He beams proudly as he applies a smidge of guyliner under my eyes. "If we weren't working tonight, I'd hire you myself."

121

In just the few short weeks I've known him, Georgie has become my best friend. He checks in with me daily with hints on how to deal with particular clients. He's been a life saver.

"You couldn't afford me." I pick at the spikes in my hair for the tenth time.

"Stop that." Georgie swats my hand away. "And I could totally afford you. But you wouldn't make me pay."

"Is that so?" I look him up and down and shrug. "I've seen better."

"Well, now you're just lying." He smacks my ass through the leather shorts I'm wearing. "Cuz there ain't nothing as fine as Georgie's behind."

Dear god. He's rhyming. "Whatever. But I can't wear these boots."

"Oh, you will wear those boots and you'll like em." He bends down and unties the huge combat boots that I think look ridiculous with shorts. "You just didn't lace them right. That's why they're chaffing."

"What time is it?" The bachelor party is expected to arrive by midnight but we're supposed to be in the suite by eleven thirty in case they come early. I'm hoping they all *come* early and I can be in bed by one.

"It's ten after so we need to hurry. Just sit still so I can fix your hair," he runs his fingers under the tap to wet them then artfully sculpts my strands, "again."

"Sorry but this shit is itchy." I hate hair gel and Georgie used half a tube to get it to his satisfaction.

"Quit yer bitchin and sit still. I swear to god I'll cut you if you don't relax."

"Down, girl." I pet his arm like a cat. "We have plenty of time."

"Pfff." Georgie wraps a black leather collar around my neck. "We haven't even discussed what our limits are."

"What are you talking about?" I glance at him through the mirror as he slips a leather vest over my arm.

"Well, we can't just walk out and start fucking each other. We need some kind of game plan." He reaches for his phone. "Where the hell are Scott and Riley. They should be here by now."

God, I didn't even think of that. I've been with friends before but Georgie has become more like a brother...or a mom to me. The thought of fucking him in front of strangers makes my stomach turn.

"Is that what they're gonna want?"

"Usually that's where it starts." Just as Georgie starts thumbing out a nasty gram, the elevator dings to the penthouse. "That must be them."

Thirty seconds later, two hot young men walk into Georgie's room. "You bitches ready."

Scott and Riley are wearing the same outfit as me. Georgie finally drops his robe and reaches for the matching shorts he's laid out on the bed. His body is lean and soft with a beautifully shaped cock.

I can't stop myself from watching as he slides his shorts up and adjusts his soft penis artfully against his pelvis so the outline is clearly visible through the fabric. I step back and check out my own package in the mirror.

I didn't notice earlier but my mushroom head and thick shaft are pointed down and almost peeking out the hem of the shorts. Nothing is left to the imagination. If I sit down, you'll see my slit peeking out from between the leather and my thigh. This should be an interesting night.

Chapter Twelve

Patton

When I agreed to let Finn stay at my place, I didn't realize that included picking him up at the airport at eight AM.

"Sorry but it was the cheapest flight I could get," Finn says as he tosses a duffle bag in the back of my Durango.

"It's fine." I am usually up early anyway but setting an alarm on a non-work day is sacrilege. I didn't have any clients so I took the day off to be a good host. Just because he's a complete douche, doesn't mean I need to be rude.

Aria Grace

"I'm starving." Finn pulls out a Snickers from his pocket then turns to me. "You eat yet?"

"No." I pull out of the airport then head toward I-205. "You want to stop somewhere or just get a bagel or something from my house?"

"Well, I'm saving my money for tonight but if you want to stop somewhere, that's cool."

God, was he always like this? I can't remember what I actually saw in him. "Yeah, that's fine. I know a place that usually isn't too busy."

We have a quick breakfast before Finn pretends not to notice the check being dropped. I leave some cash and we head toward my place. Dropping him off at the airport tomorrow will definitely be the highlight of my weekend.

Finn isn't used to being awake before noon so as soon as we get inside my apartment, he informs me that he's taking a nap and makes himself comfortable on my bed. I use the time to go for a run and do some laundry. Not exactly exciting but since I have the day off, I might as well make the most of it.

Eight o'clock rolls around before I can think of a way to back out of being Finn's plus one so I put on the clothes he insists I look hot in and we climb into the limo the best man rented for the night.

"What's your poison, Pat?" Dave is mixing drinks as soon as the car is rolling.

"Do you have gin and tonic?" I scoot a few inches away from Finn. He's practically sitting in my lap. "And it's Patton."

"Coming right up, Pat Tin." He draws out my name as if it's two words. What the fuck ever.

While I sip mine, the other seven guys in the car do Jägerbombs. Most of them are buzzed before we get to Pai Men Miyake, the best Japanese restaurant in town. I'm able to stay relatively sober through the slow dinner and visit to a comedy show.

I've learned that when Finn is drinking, he's out of control. I don't want to be the babysitter but I also can't trust him to make good decisions for me if I do have a few too many.

So, I'm the sober asshole in the group of eight drunken assholes. After a comedy show that is pretty decent, I'm looking forward to heading home and crawling into bed. I've got a mild headache forming and can't stomach another drink.

"Dave, thanks again for inviting me tonight," I say when we climb into the back of the limo. "I had a great time."

"The night is still young, Pat." Derek looks at me like I'm crazy. "We haven't even gotten to the best part yet."

"Oh, fuck." Finn laughs and pulls me into his lap. "Patton is gonna turn into a pumpkin if we don't get him home before midnight."

"Fuck off." I move to the bench on the other side of Finn. "What's next?"

"It's a surprise." Derek pulls a bandana out from a duffle bag. "And Dave has to put this on before he gets out."

I hate surprises. They're never good. Learning that my uncle only let me call him daddy because he felt sorry for me was a bad surprise. Finding my mom almost dead from an overdose when I was nine was a bad surprise. And walking in on Finn sucking Jack's dick was definitely a bad surprise.

We pull into an underground parking garage and the limo stops directly in front of an elevator. After making sure Dave was properly blindfolded, everyone gets out of the limo. I'm tempted to stay inside, hoping no one notices I'm not with the group but when Derek crawls back in for the duffle bag, he drags my sleepy ass out with him.

Just wanting to get through the night, I climb in the elevator and we begin our ascent to hell on earth. At first, the room looks like a typical hotel suite with three wide couches that overlook the city and a few closed doors on the east and west walls.

The room is much neater than I would have expected from these guys but I can see why Finn didn't want to pay to stay here. It's nicer than any hotel I've ever stayed in.

Derek guides Dave to sit in the center of the room while the rest of us sit on the couches. Finn pulls my hip close to his but my head is hurting too much to bother fighting it.

There's a wet bar at the front of the room with several bottles of water visible through the glass door so without worrying about whose credit card will be charged for incidentals, I grab a bottle and take a drink.

"Water?" Finn gives me an annoyed look. "Seriously?"

I shrug. "I have a headache. You don't have any aspirin on you, do you?"

His eyebrow arches then he smiles. "I do, actually. I always bring some when I know I'm gonna be drinking."

Finn lifts one hip and sticks his hand in his pocket. He pulls out a loose white pill. It's kinda gross but I don't even care if there is pocket lint on it. I just need the pounding to stop.

Without even looking at it, I pop the pill and take a swig of my water before the four doors open in the room. The lights are slightly dimmed and four beautiful men walk out dressed in leather shorts and vests. The one in front of me has hot pink hair and is stalking me like a lion.

As my brain starts to realize what's happening, I look to my left and see two other guys crawling across the coffee table to Dave. He pulls his blindfold off just as the first guy places his palm on Dave's lap.

Then I look to the fourth man. He's on my right but not advancing as aggressively as the others. When I turn and see Caleb's slack jaw and tortured eyes, I want to bolt. And cover him up.

His pristine skin is almost completely on display for these drunk assholes. Pink hair is trying to get my attention but I shove him toward Finn and try to stand. The hurt on Caleb's face turns to anger in a split second. And it's directed at me. He rearranges his expression from one of shock to one of pure lust as he gets his head in the game.

With his crystal blue eyes barely peeking out from his white blond lashes, he stalks to me. My breathing picks up as my cock does the same. I don't want to be turned on but I can't stop my body's reaction. Without lifting a finger to stop him, Caleb climbs onto my lap, planting both knees in the cushions beside my thighs. I'm completely caged in by him and harder than I've been in a year.

Caleb slowly tilts his hips so his ass rubs the full length of my straining dick. "What a nice surprise this is."

"What are you doing here, Caleb?" My mouth is finally able to form words but my brain is still trying to catch up. Vinnie said he quit the bar and took a job with Dylan. Dylan runs an arcade. Now that the thought is at the forefront of my mind, it doesn't make much sense. *Why the hell would Caleb go to work in an arcade?*

"You know why I'm here." Caleb lets his tongue graze my lower lip then across my jaw to my earlobe. "You know I'm just a filthy whore."

"What?" I pull away as if he slapped me. "I never said that."

"Sure you did." Caleb's hands are rubbing my pecs over my shirt. "You made it very clear how you felt about my kind."

"I'm sorry about—" I try to remember the apology I've had floating in my head for weeks but Caleb cuts me off.

"Don't be." He rotates his ass above me again and slowly guides his hands down my abs. His eyes are intensely staring me down. "I guess it's okay to pay for sex...but not to get paid for it."

I can't keep my breath from hitching as his fingers skim my belly. I make a living touching others but it's been a long time since someone has touched me in even a minimally sensual way.

My head isn't pounding anymore. It's more of a dull throbbing as the music starts to relax me.

"Damn fuck it is." Finn slides his hand behind Caleb's neck and pulls him over, forcefully pressing their mouths together.

"What are you doing, Finn?" I force my arm between them to separate their lips.

"Your boyfriend just wants to have some fun." Caleb's sexy voice has an edge to it. "Don't be so uptight."

"He's not my fucking boyfriend." I hold Caleb's shoulder and tilt him toward me. "Is this really what you do?"

"It really is." His hand is now under Finn's shirt. "But I can take care of both of you. I'm a professional, you know. No need to get greedy."

"He's got a stick too far up his ass to want anything." Finn glances at his watch. "At least not for a few more minutes."

Caleb pulls back and looks at Finn. "What's that supposed to mean?"

"Don't worry about him, beautiful." Finn starts to unbutton his pants. "You've got a willing customer right here."

Caleb's eyes flick to mine for just a second before his face morphs back into the sex pot that he wants us to see. "I'm here to please," Caleb purrs as he slides off Finn's lap and lands on the floor between his legs.

I want to be pissed. I am pissed but I'm also hot as hell. I lean back and watch the show beside me, trying to find the righteous indignation I know is just below the surface of my tingling skin.

Chapter Thirteen

Caleb

Seeing Patton at the end of the couch almost stopped my heart. He doesn't look comfortable here and if the horrified expression on his face when he sees me is even a small hint at what he's feeling, I want to throw up.

But whether I like it or not, I chose this job for a reason. I need to make money and put myself through school. That's it. I don't do it because I'm a nympho and I don't do it because I don't think I'm capable of anything else. I know I'm damn well capable of great things but until I have a degree and some money in the bank, I can't do any of them.

Patton can think whatever he wants of me. He thinks he's better than me. He's probably right. Good for him. I never claimed to be a saint so he can just suck it up and deal.

With his friend's sheathed dick in my mouth, I can completely tune out everyone else. We were hired to entertain this group and that's what I'm going to do.

With a quick peek to my right, I see a dark skinned man pinning Georgie to the wall while Scott rides him from behind. It's erotic as fuck but I don't spend time watching them. I'm much more aware of the man to my left. His hard-on is a direct contradiction to the frightened expression on his face.

After a few minutes of sucking him off, I want to get this show on the road so I slip my finger below his balls and find his eager opening. Finn turns to Patton before grabbing his shirt and pulling him to his mouth. Patton is still for a second but quickly pulls off his friend.

"Don't touch me, Finn." He wipes his mouth with his palm. "When you decided to fuck Jack, you made the choice to never touch me again."

"God, you're a pussy." He turns to the guy on his left and pulls him in for a kiss. That guy is being fucked by Riley and doesn't mind Finn's forceful mouth. As soon as they connect, Finn unloads in the condom. I let him ride out his orgasm within the suction of my mouth. As soon as he's soft, I pull off and take the rubber with me, discreetly tossing it into a corner.

Having spent, Finn seems content to work his friend with his hand so I turn back to Patton. The beautiful man is watching me with glassy eyes. His smile is lazy and predatory at the same time.

Something has definitely changed from his disgusted attitude just a few minutes ago.

"Is it my turn?" He scoots to the edge of the couch and wraps his long legs around my ass, caging me in.

"You want a turn?"

"After watching what you did to Finn, I think I deserve one." He leans into me and kisses me hard. My jaw is slack from shock so his tongue slips in easily and begins its assault on mine. I want to respond but I know something's wrong.

Finn looks at us and his eyes widen. "Oh, you're ready."

He shoves me away and sprawls across Patton's chest, kissing him while trying to pull his shirt off.

It takes me a minute for my mind to catch up.

"What did you do to him?" I'm trying to remain calm but as each second ticks by, my patience is wearing thinner.

Finn doesn't respond. His hand is fully inside Patton's jeans while Patton's head is thrown back on the couch with his eyes closed.

"Hey, fuck head!" I grab the back of Finn's hair and pull him up so he's looking at me. "What did you do to him?"

"I just gave him a happy pill. Chill the fuck out, man. He's loving it."

Patton does seem to be loving it. But I know he wouldn't let this happen if he was lucid so I pull Finn to the ground and lean over Patton. "Hey, Patton."

His eyes half open and his face splits into a perfect smile. "There you are." He reaches for my dick. "Is it my turn yet?"

Fuck. I take a look around the room and everyone is engaged with at least two other people except Finn. He's still glaring at me.

"Fine, have him." Finn crawls over to Riley and wraps his hands around his hips. "But you're not getting a fucking tip from me."

What the fuck ever. I gently shove Patton's hands off me then walk to Georgie.

"I know this guy and he's been drugged." Georgie pulls his mouth off the guy he's working on long enough to see where I'm pointing. With the throbbing cock nuzzled against his cheek, he nods to me.

"Do what you need to do." His tongue flicks the man's seeping tip. "But call Marco and tell him what you're doing."

I lean down and place a kiss on his head. "Thanks, man."

He pats my calf then turns his attention back to his eager client.

Patton has his hand in his jeans and is leaning close to Riley's face. Fuck. I've got to get him out of here before he does something I'll regret. I mean, he'll regret.

I grab the house phone then slide on the couch between Patton and the fuckfest next to him. His eyes light up when he sees me. "You're back for me."

"Yeah, we're gonna get out of here." I dial security. "I just have to make a quick call."

Marco picks up on the first ring. "Everything okay in there?"

I laugh quietly. "Yeah, we're good. Sorry to bug you but I need to get one of the guys out of here."

"What do you mean?" I hear a heavy door close on the other side of the line so I know he's walking up the staircase. "What's going on?"

"Um, a guy I know is here and he was slipped something, probably E." I let out a deep breath, knowing how stupid this sounds. "He didn't want to be here before it kicked in so I want to get him out of here."

"Are you sure you know what he wants?" Marco is breathing heavily. He must be almost at our floor.

"I know he doesn't want to be a part of this orgy."

"Okay, I'll be there in thirty seconds to help you get him to a private room."

I stand and pull Patton with me. He's got forty pounds on me but comes willingly. As soon as he's standing, his hands are on my ass, sneaking under the edges to my bare skin. I know I shouldn't let it affect me but my dick isn't so sensible. It is fattening up at the thought of Patton's soft hands rounding my hip and touching it.

Just as I reach the front door, it opens quietly. Marco quirks an eyebrow when he sees Patton's roaming hands. "Are you sure about this?"

"Yeah, I know how it looks but I swear he's really conservative." I back Patton out of the room. "Is it okay if I clock out for the night and take him to my place?"

The smirk on Marco's face is downright insulting now. "I swear I just want to keep an eye on him until it's out of his system. Dylan knows this guy. You can call him if you don't believe me."

Dylan has been trying to get me to call Patton for a week. He'll understand.

"I believe you." Marco pops his head back in the room and takes a look around. "Everything else okay in there?"

"Yeah, everyone else is good."

He nods and walks me to the elevator. I step in with my arm around Patton's waist. He's expertly digging his thumb into the skin between my shoulder blades. "You're so tight, Caleb." He laughs but it's forced. "Well, your back is tight. Probably not other places."

"Yup, I'm a slut." I hit the button to get to my floor. "And if you don't keep your hands off me, I'm going to show you just how loose I am."

"Promise," he whispers into my ear as he grinds his crotch into my hip.

Fuck me.

~**~

As soon as we close the door to my apartment, I realize what a bad idea this is. If he's only twenty or thirty minutes into his high, we've got several more hours ahead of us. If I was smart, I would have taken him down to the gym to walk it off on the treadmill. Not that he would agree to that.

"So where are we going to do this?" His shirt is off and on the floor next to his shoes before I can stop him. He unbuttons his jeans as he's walking toward my room. "In here?"

"Um yeah." I follow slowly behind as he steps out of his boxers and turns to me, naked as the day he was born. God, he's beautiful. I want to spend the rest of the night just admiring him but I need to distract him from whatever he thinks is about to happen. "I'm thirsty. Can I get you some water?"

"Yeah, that sounds good." He crawls to the center of my bed and lays down. "Hurry back."

I've dealt with users before but I was always trying to help them maintain their high. Trying to lose one is a lot harder. I fill a glass with ice and pour a bottle of water over it.

When I return with the water, Patton is stroking his cock as he lays on his side with one knee bent and perpendicular to the bed. Good lord, what was I thinking?

I keep my eyes averted as I hand him the water. I know what he thinks he wants right now but he'll never forgive me if I give in. I'll never forgive myself.

"I have an idea." I try to sound sexy but my breath is heavy from the glimpse of his body I can't avoid. "Roll onto your stomach and let me take care of you for a little while."

"Now you're talking." He hands the glass back.

"Uh uh." I shake my head. "You drink that first and then I'll start."

He looks like he's going to roll his lower lip out but then quickly chugs the water, letting a few rogue drops escape down either side of his mouth. I have to fist my hands to keep from reaching out and wiping them off with my fingers.

"Done." He almost throws the empty glass at me then flips over and gets on all fours. His beautiful hole is staring at me, begging me to lick it.

"Okay." I turn my head and count to ten. I can do this. Placing the glass on the night stand, I press firmly on Patton's ass. "Lay down for now."

He does but looks back at me with a confused expression. Before I lose my nerve, I straddle his ass and sit at the top of his thighs. My hard cock is nestled in his crack but I figure he's gonna need something to keep him still and I deserve at least a little dry humping if I'm going to resist him for the rest of the night.

With no clue where to begin, I rub my hands together for ten seconds then place them on his shoulders.

"What are you doing?" Patton's whole body tenses under me. His whole naked body. I try not to focus on the way his ass squeezes around my cock or how his biceps flex into thick balls. And I certainly don't let myself think about any other balls.

As if this is totally normal, I keep kneading his shoulders, speaking in a soft sing-song tone. "Shhh. Just relax. I want to take care of you first."

"You want to give me a massage?" I can hear the uncertainty in his voice even as his shoulders loosen up and flatten under my fingers.

"Yeah." At least I'm gonna try. I'm trying to remember the things he did to me when I was on his table a few weeks ago but I'm too distracted by the way his blond hair lays messily on my pillow. It looks good there. "Just focus on how my hands feel on your skin. How relaxed your muscles are."

I've dealt with enough tweakers to know how to handle them. And if he's over stimulated right now, hopefully I can get him relaxed enough to pass out for a few hours and sleep it off.

"Mmmm." His moaning almost breaks my concentration but I just move down his back, drawing straight lines along his spine with my thumbs then circling back up his sides. He's still grinding into the mattress but at least he isn't pumping back up over my dick. I don't think I could handle that for very long.

I change directions so I'm sitting in the small of his back and staring down at his ass and legs. I really wish he'd close his legs so I can't see his balls peeking out at me. Ignoring them as well as I can, I rub the heel of my palms down each of his thighs to his knees then back up to the bottom of his ass.

After a few minutes on his thighs, I crawl backward and perch just behind his knees then I flip around so I'm looking at his feet. Raising his left ankle, I press my thumbs into the bottom of his feet from his arch to his toes. Patton's feet are soft and smooth. He must always wear shoes because there isn't a callus or rough patch that I can feel. I'm tempted to take his toes in my mouth and nip at each one but my goal is to get him to sleep, not to get myself hard again.

By the time l lower his left foot, his breathing has evened out and I'm confident he's asleep. Not in any hurry to rush off him, I gently raise his right foot and give it the same treatment. Even in his sleep, Patton makes soft moaning sounds that give me more satisfaction than I've had from any sexual encounter in a long time. I wonder if this is how he feels with every client. If so, I may have to take some massage classes.

When I can't think of any more excuses to stay on his naked body, I slowly climb off and throw a blanket over him. I don't want him too warm and cozy or the high will last longer but I don't want him to be uncomfortable while he's sleeping.

He's gonna feel like shit for at least a day or two as it is. Might as well have one good night before it wears off. And I don't hate the idea of him having happy memories of being in my bed.

I pull a pair of sweats from my dresser and quietly slip out of the ridiculous leather shorts I'm still wearing. As I'm reaching for a shirt, I hear his deep voice whispering to me.

"Why are you getting dressed, Caleb?" I freeze mid reach and glance over my shoulder. Patton's eyes are black as they trail over me. "I'm still waiting for you to finish what you started."

I pull on a t-shirt before fully turning back to him. "Just rest for a little while and then we'll talk."

He lifts up on his elbows and tries to shake his head but he's wobbly. "I don't want to talk. I want to fuck. You."

Why am I not driving my dick up his ass right this second? I have no idea.

Knowing it's wrong and stupid, I walk to the bed and sit beside him with my back against the headboard. "You don't want to. And definitely not with me. Just take a nap and you'll feel better."

I know that's a lie but we're only a few hours in and I don't think I can resist him for much longer if he's awake.

"Of course I want you." He leans over and rests his face on my thigh, running his fingers lightly over my belly. My abs quiver as his light touch passes over each muscle. "I've wanted you since I saw you in the bar. Are you still mad at me?"

"I'm not mad at you." I blow out a deep breath, causing some of his thick strands to flutter against his neck. "But you didn't want to be here tonight and I don't think you willingly took whatever Finn gave you so until you're thinking straight and feeling good, nothing is going to happen."

I leave out the part about how disgusted and repulsed he'll be once he's no longer under the influence. No sense in getting him upset now. He'll be pissed off enough in the morning to make up for it.

I run my fingers through his hair until he falls asleep in my lap.

Chapter Fourteen

Patton

Am I dead? If I'm not, can I be? It takes me a minute to remember why the sheets feel like silk. When I crack an eyelid, I realize they are. I'm in a luxury apartment that I shouldn't be in.

I bolt straight up and look around. Caleb isn't anywhere to be seen. Neither are my clothes. The room is dark but the pile of folded clothes on a chair looks vaguely familiar so I slowly get out of bed and walk toward it.

Everything is folded neatly and my shoes are lined up under the chair. He's a thoughtful prostitute, I'll give him that.

As soon as I notice the open bathroom door, my bladder screams for release. Still feeling a bit nauseous, I sit on the toilet to piss. I need to close my eyes or I might puke. The imminent sickness passes after a few minutes with my forehead pressed up against the vanity countertop. Once I'm able to stand without swaying, I quickly get dressed and head toward the living room.

The windows aren't covered in here so the bright morning sun is almost blinding. Apparently this is an Eastern facing window. As soon as my eyes adjust, I see Caleb sitting at the oak dining table with a laptop and several textbooks laid out in front of him.

He looks up with an unreadable expression. I can feel my face burning with humiliation from all that I said and did last night. I've never been so wanton. Just thinking about how I threw myself at him so many times, I want to crawl into a hole and never come out.

Once we make eye contact, my belly clenches. I want to look away but I can't. His blue eyes seem to be searching for something from me but I don't know what. The only thing I can offer is an apology.

"Thanks for getting me out of there last night." I finally pull away from his gaze and reach for my wallet. "What do I owe you? I've, um, never done this before."

His face quickly becomes very readable. And very angry. "Fuck you, Patton."

"What?" Did I say something wrong? "I don't want to stiff you. I just don't know what you charge for…"

"Consider it a comp." Caleb wraps his hands around the edge of the table and stands, leaning forward like he's trying not to jump over it and punch me in the face. "Now get the fuck out of my home before I call security and have you removed."

I raise my hands in submission and back away. "Okay, sorry."

Without another word, I leave Caleb's apartment and head to the street to find a cab.

~**~

Finn is the last person I want to see when I open my front door. Unfortunately, his naked ass is on my couch so I can't exactly avoid him. Without waking him up, I head straight to my bedroom. I feel like shit and the only thing that I can bear the thought of is a nap.

It seems like my eyes have barely closed before Finn is glowering above me.

"What?" I pull a pillow over my head.

"What happened to you last night?" He's got the balls to yell at me? "If you didn't leave your keys in the limo, I would have had to sleep on your porch."

"Get your shit together." I get up from the bed with my back to him. "I'm taking you to the airport now."

"We don't need to leave for a few hours." He picks up a picture of my mom on my dresser. It was taken at my high school graduation. One of the last times I saw her clean.

"Put it down and get your shit. We're leaving now." I stand and walk out of the room.

"What the fuck is your problem, man?" He follows and places his hand on the bathroom door so I can't close it. "You should be thanking me for getting you some action."

"By drugging me?" I grab a handful of his shirt and back him against the hallway wall. "You fucking know I don't do that shit."

"Sorry." He looks apologetic for the first time since I've known him. Even after I caught him with Jack, he was more annoyed at being caught than repentant. He was probably high at the time. "I just thought you needed to chill out and have some fun. You got a private party with that twink so what's your fucking problem?"

I want to punch him but I can't even look at him. Not only is anger rolling my stomach but so is shame. I can't believe Caleb saw me at my absolute worst and I still managed to insult him.

Without another word to Finn, I turn on my heel and walk into the bathroom. With the door locked, I get undressed and step into a steaming shower. I feel dirty all over and just want to cleanse the mortification from my pores.

~**~

The ride to the airport is silent. I don't even say goodbye when I pull up to the curb at the Southwest gate. Finn turns to me for a hug or some kind of acknowledgement but I keep my eyes straight ahead, unwilling to give him the satisfaction of a parting glance. If I never see him again, that'll be too soon.

I'm just pulling into the parking lot when my phone rings. I'm tempted to ignore it but when I see my aunt's name on the screen, I reluctantly answer.

"Patton, it's your auntie." My aunt Julie is more like my mother than my aunt. I'm not in the mood to catch up but the crack in her voice makes me nervous.

"Hi, Auntie. Is everything okay?" I pull into my spot in the carport and hold my breath. "Is it Mom?"

"I'm so sorry, ku`uipo." Her voice is now a shuddering sob. "We couldn't save her this time."

I close my eyes and lean my forehead on the steering wheel. I've known this call would come someday. Since I was nine years old, I knew the drugs would take her. It was only a matter of time.

"When?" I whisper.

"Last night." Aunt Julie clears her throat and is speaking in a calm tone. "Her friends called an ambulance but it was too late."

I nod even though she can't see me. After a long silence, I find my voice. "Should I come home?"

I visited her in Kauai for Thanksgiving and really don't want to go back. But I don't want to leave my aunt to deal with everything on her own.

"No." She always knows what the right thing to do is. She took me and Mom in when I was a baby and always made sure I was safe. She never gave up on my mom, even when she should have. "She wanted to be cremated so we'll do a small memorial in March on her birthday. That's what she would have wanted."

After feeding my aunt some lies about how great things are and how happy I am, I zombie walk into my apartment and toss my phone on the kitchen counter. I'm done thinking and feeling for the day. Now I just want to sleep.

When I wake up again, it's dark out. My alarm says six but my body feels like I've been asleep for a week. I'm achey and stiff in all the wrong places.

Forcing myself out of bed, I make a sandwich and flip on the TV. There's a Pawn Stars rerun that I let myself get sucked into.

Cold cereal and cold sandwiches are all that I have the energy to prepare and even those simple dishes seem like too much trouble most of the time.

As much as I don't want it to, my mind keeps replaying my night with Caleb. The way his warm hands worked my muscles. The way his hard dick was pressed against my crack for the entire time he straddled me. *Holy fuck, he straddled me.*

My dick twitches at the memory but not enough to fully harden. I couldn't even jack off if I wanted to. Much like a hot meal, it's not worth the trouble.

When my alarm goes off at eight on Monday morning, I feel even worse than yesterday. I'm tempted to call in sick but since I took Saturday off, I really can't. So, I trudge through the day with polite indifference toward everyone I meet. My clients are satisfied and probably just think I'm quiet for their benefit. That works for me.

Days pass in a blur of work and home. A week after the call about my mom, a fast rapping on my door wakes me from my TV fog. I hit the mute button and pretend I'm not home.

"Patton, open the door." Heather is calling me through the door. "I know you're home."

Not willing to be intentionally rude, I pull myself up from the couch and trudge to the door. I run my palm down the front of my shirt to straighten it but it doesn't help any. I put on this shirt Saturday morning and it's now Sunday afternoon. I think.

"Hi, Heather." I paste on a fake smile when I open the door and wait for her to tell me why she's here. "What brings you by?"

"I just wanted to check on you." She and Charlie Ann squeeze past me and into my apartment. I take a look around for the first time in days and am embarrassed about how I've been living...or not living.

"I'm sorry about the mess." I grab some empty beer bottles and coffee cups from the table and place them on the breakfast bar. "I've been a little busy."

"Busy with what?" Her eyes don't miss a thing. She's scrutinizing my unkempt appearance and stuffy apartment as if it's offending her. "What's going on with you?"

"Just some family stuff." I haven't shed a tear since I got the news about Mom but with a compassionate person actually asking about me—caring about me—I can't hold back the emotion. "My mom died last week."

"Oh my god, Patton." Heather puts Charlie on the floor at her feet and walks into my chest. "I'm so sorry, honey."

Now that the tears are flowing, I can't pull them back. I don't think I've ever openly sobbed in front of anyone as an adult but I can't stop. Heather holds me and rubs my back while my tears wet her shoulder. After a minute of heavy tears, I feel a thousand pounds lighter and am able to compose myself.

Charlie is wrapped around my leg so as soon as Heather pulls back, I lift the sweet girl into my arms and hold her to my chest. Her fresh baby smell is comforting and I inhale deeply, letting it calm me.

"Let's sit." Heather guides me to the sofa and cuddles into my side with Charlie in my lap. "Is there anything I can do for you? Do you need to go back to Colorado?"

I shake my head and wipe my wet eyes. "No. She lived in Kauai but we aren't doing a service until March so I'm not going yet."

Charlie's chubby fingers pound on the remote she pulled from between the cushions. When sound returns to the TV, Heather and I both startle.

"Charlie, leave that alone." Heather pulls the remote from her hand and turns off the TV.

"I'm sorry I broke down like that." I peek up at Heather as my cheeks fill with heat. "I never cry."

She rests her head on my shoulder. "Well, that's your problem. You obviously needed to let go of some of your grief. You can't just bottle it up."

I don't know how to respond so I sit quietly with the only two people in this town that give a shit about me.

After a while, Heather grabs the remote and starts flipping channels. Shrek is just starting so she turns it on and Charlie lays next to me with her head on my lap.

"You got any food in this place or should we order in?"

Surprised by her question, it takes me a minute to inventory the fridge in my head. I haven't been shopping so there isn't much. "We should probably order something if you guys are staying. Maybe pizza or Chinese?"

"Cheap Chinese delivers." She pulls out her phone and starts flipping through her contacts.

"Um, how cheap are we talking?" I fake a smile. "I don't want to get sick or anything."

"Don't worry." She waves a hand in my direction. "Dylan and I eat it all the time. It's really good. They just have a bad name."

Just the mention of Dylan's name makes my stomach clench. He's called several times over the past week but hasn't left a message. I figure if he has something important to say, he'll say it to the machine. Until then, I'm going to avoid him like I've been doing to every other guy I've met in this town.

After Heather finishes placing the order online, I turn to her. "Um, do you know much about where Dylan works?"

Heather scrunches her face and furrows a brow. "Not that much. It's some big arcade downtown.

He just got a promotion so he's there like 24/7. Between work and Spencer, I hardly talk to him anymore."

I just nod and turn toward the TV. It's not my place to tell Heather her brother is some kind of pimp. A high end one, but a pimp nonetheless.

Chapter Fifteen

Caleb

When Dylan asked about what happened with Patton, I gave him the short version of our night. It was all essentially true but I left out the parts about how badly I wanted to fuck Patton when he stripped out of his clothes and lay across my bed. And I definitely didn't mention how much it fucking hurt when he offered to pay me the next morning.

I know I'm a whore by definition but I can count on one hand the number of times I've been treated like one. Most of my tricks are friends, or at least act like a friend with benefits, and care about my comfort and pleasure to some degree. Ron is the recent exception but I couldn't care less about him. He's got a lot of issues and not being able to find someone to fuck him for free is just one of them. I feel more pity for him than anything else.

But Patton was different. He reached out to me with completely pure intentions. A little too pure for my liking but at least he was honest. He never asked for anything from me and that was my undoing. Being liked and cared for was such a foreign concept that I let my mind run away with the fantasy.

I conned myself into believing he could be something serious. Someone that would be around for a while. I let myself forget that sleeping with several men every other night didn't exactly make me boyfriend material.

When Dylan asked if we were together, I couldn't keep the sadness out of my voice when I responded with a simple no. He didn't press me on it. He knows what I do and why I'll be single for the foreseeable future.

It's been a week now and I'm still pissed but I can't stop thinking about Patton. Every time I'm with a client, I can't keep Patton's bronzed face from popping into my head. Whether or not I come, he's definitely helped me stay hard.

And when I'm alone and have access to any porn on the internet, it's still his beautifully sculpted body that drives me over the edge every fucking time.

Dylan has been checking on me daily so when his afternoon call comes in, I answer without thought. "Hey, boss. What's up?"

"Get dressed and meet me at my car. We're getting Chinese."

"We are?" I look at the clock. It's almost six so dinner sounds okay. I didn't eat lunch and my stomach rumbles at the thought of food. "Um, okay, but why?"

"I'm hungry. Aren't you?"

"Yeah, I guess." I hang up and close my laptop.

Dylan has never asked me out to eat, and definitely not just the two of us. I change my shirt then run some gel through my hair as I think about what his real reason could be. Did I do something wrong? Did he get a complaint about me? After replaying every hour I've worked over the past few days, nothing stands out as an issue.

I'm suddenly less hungry when I realize I might have said Patton's name out loud the other day when I was with a new client. I didn't think he heard me and it didn't seem to slow him down but maybe he was offended and filed something with management. Fuck me. If I lose this job, I lose my apartment too. I know Ray would let me go back there but finding a cheap apartment on short notice will be tough.

I'm biting chunks out of my cuticles when I enter the parking garage. Dylan is already leaning against his white Lexus. His dark curls fall artfully around his face. He's growing it out longer than when I first met him but I'm guessing his sexy smart boyfriend has something to do with that. Maybe Spencer likes something to hold on to. Not that Dylan's stacked muscles wouldn't provide more handholds than a jungle gym.

"Caleb, good to see you." Dylan ducks into the car as soon as I reach the passenger side so I climb in after him.

"Hi." I close the door and get settled in the seat without looking at him. If he has something to say, he'll say it when he's ready.

"Why do you look like you're about to puke?" He taps my shoulder to get me to look at him. "You feeling okay?"

I nod. "Yeah, just a little surprised to get your call."

"Oh, that?" He pulls out of the garage and zips into evening traffic. "My sister called and asked me to bring her some food. I figured you could use the fresh air."

"Um, okay." As soon as we pull into the Cheap Chinese parking lot, my stomach rumbles loudly.

Dylan laughs and turns off the car. "Sounds like I'm just in time."

I've been eating here at least three nights a week since I moved to Portland. Dylan must also like it because he ordered enough to feed a football team. When we walk to the register in the back, there are three bags full of food just waiting for us.

The ride to his sister's apartment is short—just a few blocks away from my old place. I grab the bags and follow him blindly up the stairs. Just smelling the food in the car was torture so now I can't think of anything but digging into the garlic noodles. I have to avoid garlic when I'm working so I like to take advantage of nights off when they occur. I wonder if Dylan ordered anything with onions.

When the door opens, a pretty woman answers. I can tell she's Dylan's sister by her greyish blue eyes and perfect features.

"Thank god. I'm starving." She tosses the door open and stands with her arm extended, welcoming us in. "Just put everything on the breakfast bar."

I drop the bags and turn to introduce myself. "Hi, I'm Caleb. You must be Heather."

She takes my hand and gives me a slow look up and down. Then she looks to Dylan. "Why? Why do you get the best ones?"

He chuckles quietly and puts his arm on my shoulder. "The superior gender has to stick together."

I finally look around the room and gasp when I see Patton on the couch with a sleeping baby across his lap. I'm immediately caught in his gaze but eventually force myself to look down. The little girl doesn't look like him but it's hard to deny the domestic scene in front of me.

I can't speak. Patton finally lifts the little girl's head from his thigh and gently lowers it to the sofa. His confused expression matches my own when he turns to Heather then Dylan.

After a few more seconds of awkward silence, Heather breaks the spell we're all under.

"Patton's mother just died and he shouldn't be alone." Her words are rushed and very factual as she pulls out paper plates from a cabinet.

"Heather." Patton's face turns pink either from embarrassment or betrayal. Having seen that look before, I'm betting on the latter. "You called them?"

"You need to grieve and get back to life. You can't be alone in here for another week."

Dylan walks to Patton and wraps his arms around him. "I'm so sorry to hear that, man."

Patton closes his eyes for a moment and returns the embrace. An irrational jolt of jealousy shoots through me. As if I have anything to be jealous of. I've fucked five guys in the past three nights so a hug is hardly on the list of gestures too intimate for friends.

When he opens his eyes, they lock with mine. I take a deep breath then walk to Patton. Dylan pulls away and gives us the illusion of privacy in the small and crowded room.

It takes me a minute to find the words that I should say. There are a lot of words that I want to say but none seem right. Eventually, I hold out my hand. "I'm sorry for your loss."

Patton looks at my outstretched arm with hurt written all over his face. He awkwardly shakes it but then pulls me into his arms. "I'm sorry for everything."

Not wanting to rehash anything in our past, I just nod into his shoulder and give him a brief hug.

"Don't worry about it." I pat him one last time then back away. "We're cool."

"Really?" His face relaxes and I see a genuine smile for the first time since he was drugged and naked in my bed. The lines that were etched in his forehead just a few minutes ago are gone, replaced by smooth, bronze skin. "So we can start over?"

I shrug awkwardly. "I guess. You know what I do so it's really up to you to decide if you can be my friend."

Patton has that hurt face again. The one that makes me want to cuddle him and tell him everything will be okay. "Did you think I didn't want to be your friend because you're a... Because of your job?"

I have to laugh. That's a joke, right? "Well, let's see." I tap my finger on my chin in a dramatic way. "You gave some random soliloquy about how you hate being compared to street walkers during our first real conversation. Then you ran out of the bar when you saw me with Kevin and after I refused to take advantage of your heightened state last week, you pulled out your wallet like I was just doing it for a tip."

As I quietly list off his offenses, I can't help getting a little upset again.

Faster than I expect, Patton's fingers wrap around my elbow and he pulls me closer. His eyes are begging for forgiveness but mine keep flicking to his lips. They're so full and red and close.

"I'm so sorry, Caleb." He breathes out the words as if they're coming from the depths of his being. "I was ignorant and a hypocrite and I don't deserve to be your friend....but I'd like to be."

As I process his words, my head nods in acceptance. I can handle that. I don't have a lot of friends that I just hang out with so we can do this.

"No more secrets or lies by omission?" Patton's hopeful expression is too cute for me not to smile.

"No more secrets." I pull him into a hug this time and hold him tightly. "Besides, I pulled my rotator cuff the other day and it's been killing me."

"How?" he asks then quickly shakes his head. "Never mind. Just make an appointment and I'll see what I can do."

"You two gonna eat or what?" Heather is standing with a set of chopsticks in her mouth. "Cuz this isn't gonna last long."

"Let's go." Patton nudges me forward. "I've seen her eat and she doesn't leave a crumb."

"I'm a growing girl." Heather's plate is piled high with noodles and beef and veggies.

Just looking at it makes my stomach rumble again. Apparently my appetite is back.

Chapter Sixteen

Patton

I can't believe Caleb wants to be my friend. I was prepared to take a punch to the gut when he walked to me but I should have known he'd only offer compassion and forgiveness. He's a genuinely good person and I've treated him like a second-class citizen. As if his occupation is the only thing that defines who he is.

Once we finally sat down to eat, I really enjoyed laughing and just being one of the guys.

It's been a long time since I've had a good guy friend that I wasn't dating. Usually my non-sexual friends are girls. I think I gravitate toward women because it's safe. There are no expectations of a relationship so the pressure's off.

With Dylan, Caleb and Heather, I'm not the guy that can give them a loan or a massage. I'm not the guy to go to for a booty call. I'm just a friend that needed company and they came together. I'm almost teary when Heather announces it's time to take Charlie home and the guys decide to leave with her.

Watching Dylan and Caleb from my window, I wish for the thousandth time I had Caleb's number. The urge to send a *thanks for coming* text is strong but when ten thirty rolls around, my phone flashes with something even better. Just before I step into the shower, I receive a *I had a great time tonight* text from Caleb.

Those six words have me floating. Not only do I finally have a number for him but now I know he's thinking of me. I know it's probably just his empathy for my grief but a selfish part of me wants to believe he's thinking of me in the same way I'm thinking of him.

I step into the steamy shower and lean against the back wall, letting the hot water cleanse me of the guilt and sorrow I've been carrying. With my hips slightly tilted upward, the pulsating water hits my cock in a rhythm I don't want to interrupt. Without realizing it, I'm thrusting in the air like a horny dog. I've been trying not to replay my night with Caleb in my head because of the shame associated with it. But now that we're friends again, I don't feel as guilty playing out the fantasy I wanted to occur that night.

I wanted him to rub my back and ass, slipping his fingers down my crack and across my balls. If he had cupped my balls for even a few seconds, I would have shot my load onto the sheets like a teenager.

With just a gentle squeeze of his hot palm, my ass would have been in the air, begging for him to attack it. I wanted him to fuck me hard. Make me feel it in my chest. Make me appreciate the experience he's gained from years as a sex worker instead of feeling sadness and disappointment over it. I wanted so much from Caleb.

If I'm being honest, I still do. I want to be confident enough that I can date a man whose job is to sleep with other people on a daily basis. But I just can't do it. I've always been the jealous type and don't know how to change that. I'm not even sure I want to change that. Just like I want to be the only person to touch my man, I want him to be possessive of me too. I want him to kick the ass of any guy who even looks at me twice. I want to be his only one.

~**~

The next month flies by. Caleb never came back for a massage but we shoot pool at Ray's or go out to lunch at least twice a week. He works most nights but when he has time off, we usually hang out.

Our friendship is stronger but so is my attraction. When I think about the guys that get to touch that creamy white skin and run their fingers through his silky hair, it pisses me off. But it pisses me off even more that I'm too chicken shit to get in the damn line.

As I'm waiting for him to meet me for a drink at Ray's, I'm also starting to stew. Why the fuck shouldn't I get a piece of him like everyone else? I'm a grown man. If I want to pay for sex, I'm allowed to. Who's gonna judge me? Caleb? He's never said a negative word about his clients in the past so why would I be any different?

I see him walk in and greet his ex-coworkers with a smile and a hug. As those beautiful eyes seek me out, I make my decision.

"I'm sorry I'm late." He bumps my fist then slides into the seat across from mine. "Traffic was a bitch."

"How much do you charge?" I didn't plan to blurt it out like that but there's no taking the words back now that they're out there.

"What?" His smile is gone and confusion is written all over his face. "Why?"

"I'm interested." I don't know what else to say. I briefly considered saying it was for a friend but lying isn't my specialty. And Caleb isn't stupid. He'd know that line of bullshit immediately.

"Oh, well, it depends on what's involved but usually a few hundred bucks." His face is red and he's clearly trying to maintain a neutral expression but there's no hiding the discomfort he feels.

"Would you take me on as a client?" I don't know if he has veto power but if he doesn't want to see me professionally, I can respect that. When he doesn't respond within three seconds, I feel my face flush and I have to look away. A man can only take so much rejection.

"It's not that I wouldn't want to but I don't understand why you would want to." When I don't look back at him, Caleb kicks the side of my foot. "Look at me."

I don't fully turn my head but with just a glance at Caleb's face, I can tell he's better composed. I run my hand through my hair and wait for him to say something. I'm fresh out of stupid questions.

"Why would you want to?" He repeats the question I can't answer.

I shrug when words don't emerge from my mouth but I can't look away from him. He's so perfectly handsome when he's curious.

"I'd be stupid not to." He's studying me with the hint of a smile forming.

Eventually, he nods. "Okay, sure."

As soon as we say goodbye at the door, I pull up the Paddle's website on my phone. Caleb explained how to find the reservation system but didn't give me more than cursory details about what to expect.

After almost dropping my phone at the rates, I order a two hour session with Caleb on Friday night. That gives me two days to psyche myself up for my first rendezvous with a hooker.

Unfortunately, two days was enough to make me almost cancel at least seven times. I'd never admit this out loud but the biggest reason I didn't back out was the fifty percent cancellation charge. If I'm gonna drop several hundred dollars for a fuck, I'm gonna damn well show up for it.

At nine o'clock, I arrive at Paddles with a bottle of wine. The security officer politely holds back his laughter when he looks at the bottle. Ignoring him, I say I'm meeting with Caleb Forester. He checks my ID then sends me up to the fourth floor. I'm a little disappointed that we aren't going to Caleb's private apartment but I don't dwell on it. There are probably protocols he needs to follow so I thank the gentleman and head to the elevator.

Caleb is standing outside the doors when they slide open. He always looks good but his hair looks a shade lighter than when I saw him in the dark bar a few days ago and his tight jeans make my own a little tighter.

"Patton." He pulls me into a quick hug then ushers me toward room 402. "It's good to see you."

Not knowing proper *first time with a prostitute* etiquette, I just grunt and hold out the bottle. "I brought wine."

"Thanks." Caleb takes it and inspects the label. "I haven't tried this but it sounds good."

Again, words escape me. When we walk into the suite, Caleb goes straight to the kitchen. "Can I pour you a glass?"

"Yes, please." Now that we're actually inside the private space, I feel a little more at ease. I don't feel like there are as many eyes watching me. Then, my eyes look to each corner of the room. "Are there cameras in here?"

Caleb laughs. "No, why? You planning to harvest my organs or something?"

"Just making sure." I take a seat on the sofa and wait for him.

"Here ya go." Caleb hands me a glass of the Merlot and sits beside me. "What shall we toast to?"

I think for a minute. "Friends with benefits?"

He scrunches his nose. "No. How about to first times?"

I smile and raise my glass, clinking it against his. "To first times."

CHAPTER SEVENTEEN

CALEB

I didn't actually think Patton would make the reservation but having him here in the flesh has my stomach in knots. I have mixed feelings about being with him. On the one hand, I've wanted to fuck him since he first sat in the stool across from me. His dark eyes seem to harbor so much love and tenderness. I just wanted to hold him and make him forget about everyone before me.

On the other hand, once he's a client, I don't think we can go back. Not that there's anything in particular to go back to. Sure, we can be friends that have sex. I'm friends with a lot of my clients. Some from before they hired me but most I got close to after I worked for them. But with Patton, it's different. I can't explain exactly why it doesn't feel like it's supposed to happen this way but the knowledge is burning in my gut.

We've managed to avoid the elephant in the room with small talk but now that our glasses are empty, we need to actually talk.

"So why are you really here?" I ask.

Patton is startled by the question but doesn't look away from me.

"Because I want to be with you and this is the only way that can happen." His words are quiet, almost whispered.

"Why do you think that?" I rest my hand on his knee. "This isn't the only way."

He nods and leans forward, resting his head in his palm. "It is for me. I want something you can't give me so this is the only way I can get a piece of you."

I smirk. "Which piece do you want?"

His eyes flick to my chest then back to the floor. "Do we have to have this conversation?"

"Yes, I think we do." I shake his knee a little and try to lighten the mood. "Consider this the consultation you aren't paying for. I just want to understand what you want."

"I want to have sex with you," he says in a rushed breath.

"That's it?" The tinge of disappointment in my voice isn't lost on him.

Patton lifts his hand to my cheek. "No, that's not it. But that's all I can afford."

"What does that mean?" I pull away from his hand.

"If I could afford...um...exclusivity...I'd pay for it." He gives me a shy smile. "But you've seen my apartment. I'm not exactly a high roller."

It takes me a minute to process his words. But when I finally do, I wish I had dropped the topic when he asked me to. "So you want to date me but not if I'm with other guys? Even if it's just a job?"

Patton looks as pained as I feel. "I know that's not possible and if I could get over it, I would. I'd at least try. But I can't imagine spending every night at home knowing my boyfriend is fucking some rich guy. It would kill me."

"Boyfriend?" What is happening?

"Well, yeah." Patton seems to shake himself back to reality. "I don't do casual sex. Well, never before tonight."

"But you came here to fuck me?" Now I'm confused. Is he just messing with me?

"Well, *be* fucked by you." His cheeks are a deep crimson as a coy smile splits his face. "But, yeah. I figured if you were okay with it, I could try."

"And then what?" I ask. "What happens tomorrow and the next day?"

"I don't know. I guess I can probably afford two or three nights a month."

"How do you do that?" I stand and walk to the window. "How do you manage to make me feel like a whore when no one else ever has?"

"I do?" Through the reflection in the glass, I can see his expression drop. He stands and is holding me before I turn around. "I'm so sorry. I never meant to offend you. I just can't get you out of my fucking head and this seemed like the only option for us."

"I can't believe you!" I feel lightheaded with the dichotomy of emotions rolling over me. I'm shocked and pissed and flattered and insulted—

all at the same time. "I think this was a bad idea. Maybe you should go."

"Really?" He steps away as if I've slapped him. "You want me to leave? Now?"

I nod, afraid of my voice trembling if I try to speak.

Patton stares at me for a full minute before finally turning away. "It seems I'm always apologizing to you. I guess this was a bad idea."

He walks out without another word.

~**~

After that night, I need a few days off to get my head together. Now that I know Patton is interested in me, or at least was interested at some point, I can't stop running different scenarios through my head. Could we give it a go? Could I be what he needs? Is he what I need?

After a few days of hosting my own pity party, Dylan stops by to kick my ass into the land of living.

"You want to tell me why you haven't left this room in the past three days?" Dylan takes a dramatic look around my apartment. "You got some poor guy tied up in the back room or something?"

I drop into a dining chair and rest my head in my hands. "I don't know what he wants from me."

"Patton?"

I give him a look as if there isn't anyone else in the world I could be talking about. I guess there isn't. "Yeah. First he hates me because of what I do. Then, he wants to be my friend. Now he wants to be a customer. What the fuck am I supposed to do with that?"

Dylan pulls a chair next to me then twists mine so we're knee to knee. "If he's just another guy in the world, the answer is pretty simple."

"It is?" This is one of those moments in life where I just need someone else to tell me what to do. I can't see beyond my hurt to think logically.

"Yes." He takes one of my hands in both of his and waits for me to meet his stare. "You just treat him like every other customer. You're friends with a lot of the guys you've worked for. It's no different."

"Then why does it feel different? Why do I feel like I can't just do my job and move on?"

Dylan raises an eyebrow and smiles. "You know the answer to that."

My shoulders fall in defeat. "Fine, maybe he is different. But that doesn't change the fact that he hates what I do and could never date me while I'm doing this."

"I can't tell you what to do." He drops my hand and leans back in his chair. "But I will tell you this. Spencer was freaked out when he found out what I do. It's different because I'm not seeing clients but it still bothered him."

"And now?" The way Spencer and Dylan are together, I can't imagine they've ever disagreed about anything. They are so completely in love that the world barely exists around them. "He's cool with it?"

Dylan chuckles lightly. "I wouldn't say he's cool but he trusts me. And if he ever asked me to leave, I'd do it in a second. Without hesitation. I know our situation is different but even if I had to take shifts at three different McDonald's to pay the rent, I'd do it in a heartbeat to keep him."

"Yeah, your situation is different. Spencer is independently wealthy so you can quit at any time. I'm not so lucky." I don't want to sound whiney but I can't help it. No matter what I do, I can't change the facts. "Even if I did quit, I don't think he could get over knowing what I used to do. He's conservative. Old fashioned."

"And you're stubborn." He pats my knee then stands. "You're never gonna be happy if you don't go for what you want. It's one thing to focus on your career and educational goals. It's entirely different to focus on your heart. But those are the goals you regret not pursuing. You'll have a lot of jobs over the course of your lifetime. Finding someone you want to be with long-term doesn't happen every day. Don't miss out on something special because you're afraid to ask for what you want."

I let his words sink in as Dylan stands to leave. He gives me a one-armed hug and kisses the top of my head. "Come by tonight for dinner."

Chapter Eighteen

Patton

Mondays are always slow but today was particularly painful. A new client came in and had every ailment in the book but wanted to really *feel* her massage. Every time I put pressure on her muscles, she squealed and explained the injury that was someone else's fault. And when I was I gentle, she bitched about not getting her money's worth.

That wouldn't have been so bad if she didn't walk in right before closing time and expect an eighty minute treatment. Had I known what a nightmare she was, I wouldn't have agreed to stay late. But I did and now I just want to collapse on my couch and tune out from the world for a few hours.

I'm so focused on placing one foot in front of the other as I walk up the stairs that I don't notice the person reading against my front door. Caleb has that same serious expression as every other time I've caught him studying.

I stand at the top step for a minute and just watch him. His hair is getting a little long and almost blocks his eyes. He's chewing on the cap of a highlighter and I can't look away from his mouth. When I realize it's no longer worrying the pen, I glance at his eyes.

They are trained on me. I take a deep breath then step toward him, deciding casual is the best way to play this. He's here for a reason so I'm going to keep my mouth shut and hear him out. Maybe then I can keep my foot out of it.

"Hi." I reach out to help him stand. "I hope you haven't been waiting long."

If someone were eavesdropping on us, they would think I was expecting him. I definitely wasn't. I was hoping it might happen someday but definitely not expecting it.

"Not too long." He wipes the dust off the back of his jeans and steps aside to let me open the door. "I didn't know when you got off."

After dropping my stuff on the counter, I grab a couple beers from the fridge and we head to the couch. "I don't know about you, but I really need one."

Caleb smiles and accepts the bottle. "Yeah, thanks."

Reminding myself to stay quiet, I take a drink and wait for Caleb to begin. After several minutes of awkward silence, he finally huffs out a breath and tilts his body so he's facing me. "I'm sorry about what happened the other night."

I want to tell him he has nothing to apologize for but I hold my tongue and just smile.

He's waiting for me to speak. When I don't, he clears his throat and folds his hands in his lap. "I think we need a do over."

"A do over?" I ask.

"I mean, if you still want to."

"I do." I tilt so now we're both angled to each other. "What do you want to do over?"

If he wants to retry our two-hour appointment, I'm more than willing. Although, we may have to wait until payday. I decide to keep that thought to myself.

"Um, everything." He's chewing his lower lip like it's jerky.

I reach out and pull his lip free with my thumb. "Okay."

"Yeah?" He leans into my hand for just a second then pulls back. "Okay, cool."

"Is this Friday good for you? I can be there any time after eight." I wiggle my eyebrows. "Unless you want to start now?"

His face scrunches in confusion and then that hurt and angry mask is back. Fuck me! Did I do it again? I should have my tongue removed for all the trouble it causes.

"Wait." I place my hands on both of his knees. "Whatever I'm not understanding, please explain to me. I don't want to piss you off...again. Just talk to me."

Caleb takes a deep breath then offers his right hand in a shake. "I'm Caleb Forester. It's nice to meet you."

Oh, okay. I'm starting to understand his visit. I take his hand. "The pleasure's mine, Caleb. I'm Patton Oliver."

"That's a firm grip you've got there, Patton," he says with a twinkle in his eye. "What do you do for a living?"

"I'm a massage therapist so I work with my hands all day." With an almost imperceptible nod, he gives me permission to ask the question I haven't had the balls to ask since I met him. "Um, what do you do for a living?"

"Well, I used to be a bartender part time and a rent boy part time." The way his chest heaves after he says the words is a clear indicator of how much stress this has been causing him.

I know I'm responsible for the stress he's been under. Clearly he was doing just fine with his decisions and his life before I came along. I feel the need to apologize again for my past behavior but two words shoot to the front of my mind. "Used to?"

"Yeah." His mouth curls into a shy smile. "Last Thursday was my last client."

"Oh." I was his client on Friday. But since nothing happened, I guess that doesn't count. Not really knowing how to respond, I try to channel Dr. Phil and go into shrink mode. "How do you feel about that?"

"Good." He chuckles at my feeble attempt to psycho analyze him. "Great, actually. I only planned to do it for a few more years anyway but now seemed like the right time to make a change."

"Why now?" I whisper. I'm not sure if I want him to say I'm part of the reason or not. That's a lot of pressure if he changed his whole life for me. We haven't even been on one date yet.

He twists so his back is against the cushions and looks toward the blank screen of my TV. He can see us in the reflection but he doesn't look directly at me. "I know why you were so disgusted at first."

"I wasn't dis—"

"Wait." He holds up a hand toward me. "Just let me finish, please."

I sit back and watch his profile as he continues.

"I've never really been in a relationship. I've dated a few guys before I started working at Ray's but nothing serious. After I started hustling, I had plenty of guys to keep me sated and I needed to focus on school and saving money. I didn't want anything more."

He quickly turns to me for acknowledgement.

"I understand." I rest my hand on his shoulder and squeeze the tense muscles. "Keep going."

"You seemed interested in me even before you knew I was a sure thing. That stirred up feelings

I've never felt before. You liked me as a person with no strings attached. And then that massage." Caleb moans a little and rests his cheek on my hand. "No one has ever taken care of me like that. Just the memory of your hands on me gets me hard."

He gasps and his cheeks flush as he looks to me. "Sorry. I didn't mean to say that. But it's true."

I can feel my own flush as I wipe my thumb across his temple. "I'm flattered."

"When you said all that stuff about not being a whore, I realized for the first time that I couldn't have the kind of relationship other people have. I was used up and untouchable. I would never be good enough for a man like you."

"That's not true," I whisper through the knot in my throat. I want him to keep going but he needs to know how wrong he is. How wrong I was.

"Anyway, when you offered to pay me for sex, a part of me was so happy to finally be getting with you. You were an active and sober participant and my fantasies would come true. But as I thought about it, I realized once you paid me, you'd always be just another customer. Another trick I see when you're in between real boyfriends."

I feel moisture on my fingers and realize a small tear has escaped his bright blue eyes. Not wanting him to misinterpret words, I do the only thing I know to comfort him.

I shift my weight so my leg slides behind Caleb's back then pull him against my chest. Once he's settled with his back nestled into my front, I wrap my arms around him and reach for his hands. Pressing my thumbs up and down his palms seems to distract him enough to keep speaking.

"I don't want you to have other boyfriends. I want you to give me a chance before you completely dismiss me." He chokes on a sob and I feel my own eyes well up at his anguish. I'd take it all on for him if I could. When I kiss the back of his neck, he stills in my arms. "But I'll understand if you can't do it."

"Can't do what?" If the hard-on I've had on and off since he arrived is any indication, I definitely *can* do it. Multiple times.

"Be with an ex-whore." I can barely hear his whisper. "I've been tested and I always used protection but that doesn't change the fact that I did it. I'll understand if you can't move past that."

I keep rubbing his hands while I consider his offer. Now that I know he isn't going to see any more clients, I can't think of any real reason not to give it a try.

"I think I can." I nuzzle into the back of his neck and place a light kiss there. "I can't bear to think of someone in your bed after I leave it so if you can promise that won't ever happen, I can promise not to hold your past against you."

Caleb nods against me and presses in closer. My dick is starting to fill at the mere suggestion of being in Caleb's bed again.

"I promise."

CHAPTER NINETEEN

CALEB

As much as I wanted him to feel this way, I didn't truly believe Patton would be open to giving us a shot at something serious. But when he turns me around and kisses me on the mouth for the first time, I feel dizzy with the endorphins flying through me.

We kissed at the bachelor party and back in my room but those weren't real. They were hot as fuck but not real. Just part of the role I was playing and a result of the drugs he took. Tonight, we're both fully engaged. His touch is soft at first and then builds pressure with each pass over mine. Like his hands work my muscles into a blob of putty, his mouth dominates mine. Our tongues do the dance of young love exploring every inch of each other.

When he pulls back for air, I chase after him, not ready to be separated. His teeth rake across my tongue then skate along my jaw. "Wanna see my room?"

I laugh and run my tongue along his ear. "Definitely."

Barely resisting the urge to run, we make it to Patton's room. He pushes me to a seated position on the bed and pulls off my shirt. In the back of my mind, I know we should take it slow but we've taken it slow enough already. I can't wait any longer.

Once my chest is bare, Patton immediately dives into me, placing desperate kisses along my clavicle and down to my right nipple.

I'm trying to stay quiet but low moans escape my throat. My dick is begging to be acknowledged but I ignore it. Right now, I'm completely focused on Patton. His gentle and attentive touch is proof that he wants to be with me. For the first time since my massage, his touch makes me feel worthy. When his tongue reaches my belly button, my ass bucks off the bed. "Oh my god, that feels good."

"Sensitive?" He smiles against my clenched abs. "What about down here?"

Patton's tongue traces the entire width of my waist band, just sneaking under the denim without getting far enough to satisfy my need.

"Yes." My breathless response is embarrassing but I don't care.

"If you say so."

Getting bold, Patton undoes the button and zipper of my jeans then slides his tongue between the open fabric. My breath stops as he makes contact with the smooth base of my cock. I'm still mostly hidden behind my pants so after a quick swipe of his tongue, Patton grabs the denim at both hips and pulls them off.

He's touched my naked body before but it wasn't like this. I was mostly covered and he had to maintain a level of professionalism. I don't think he even took a peek. Now that I'm laid bare for him, I can feel his lust rolling off him in waves.

"God, you're beautiful," he says while running a hand up my thigh.

He stands above me for a moment, just staring at me. I can't hide the wide grin on my face. "As I recall, you're not too bad yourself. Although, my memory could use a refresher."

Patton slowly undresses under my intense gaze. I've seen him strip before but he wasn't clear headed. Right now, it's all for me.

As soon as Patton is fully nude, he climbs across my body. The hot mouth I've been dreaming of for weeks meets mine. I can't remember the last time I stayed rock hard just from kissing but as the minutes pass, I realize I could probably come just from one firm thrust against his thigh.

"Do you have condoms?" I say breathlessly while he nibbles my chest.

"Yeah. In my bathroom." I like that they aren't readily accessible. Like he didn't think he'd need them any time soon.

"Get them," I say as he bites the tip of my nipple playfully. "And lube."

When he returns with the supplies, he tosses them on the bed next me. I stand and point to the edge of the bed. "Sit here."

Patton drops to the bed, watching my eyes as I kneel in front of him. "When I was giving you a massage that night, I wanted so badly to take your balls in my hands and feel their weight."

"Why didn't you?" Patton's voice trembles. "I wanted you to."

I give him as stern of a look as I can manage. This boy needs to learn when to keep his mouth shut. We both know damn well he didn't want me to, even if his body said otherwise.

Deciding to ignore the lecture brewing in my head, I duck under his cock and suck both balls into my mouth. Patton's fists burrow into the comforter to keep from thrusting against me.

My tongue draws a figure eight around his sac. His dick is beading with precum. "You're killing me, Caleb."

I slowly pull off, letting first one then the other nut drop away from my tight lips. Placing soft kisses at the base of his cock, I work my way up. When my tongue clears the moisture at his tip, my eyes close. I want to shoot right then.

"Mmm, that tastes even better than I imagined," I say reverently before wrapping my lips around his wide head and sucking. My cheeks hollow expertly as I slowly pull him into my mouth. When he hits the back of my throat, I just swallow around him, pulling Patton's cock further into the tight channel.

"Holy fuck." Patton's hand wraps around my neck and holds me there for just a second before letting go. "Sorry. Got carried away there."

I pull off, releasing the suction and smiling around his shaft. "S'okay. Want you to get carried away."

"Then keep doing that." He throws his head back and closes his eyes. "But I'm not gonna last long."

I accept that challenge. I resume sucking with vigor, massaging his length with my throat and tongue. My hand is still working his balls so I know when they tighten and pull up.

I don't let up my hold on his cock until he's poured every drop of his seed down my throat. When I finally pull away, Patton has a slightly dazed look on his face.

"Good?" I ask.

"Mmm."

"I've never tasted come before." I smack my lips together for emphasis. "It's yummy."

Patton leans up on one elbow. "Seriously? Never?"

"I told you, I always use protection."

"Even for a blow job?"

I shrug my shoulders. "Never wanted to take the risk."

When he reaches an arm out to me, I climb across his chest and rest my ear against his heart. Patton's grip tightens around me as he kisses my head. "Thank you for taking the risk with me."

Chapter Twenty

Patton

I've had some good blow jobs before but that was indescribable. The way Caleb was able to fully take every inch of me was amazing. I've never experienced anything like that. Of course, he is a fucking professional. Was, not is. But he was literally a fucking professional. And now I get the benefit of that experience. Yay me.

For a while, we just cuddle and hold each other, exploring with our hands and mouths. As soon as I start to get hard again, I slide down to Caleb's cock and pull my flattened tongue along his length. His pink head is a perfect mushroom shape as I taste the slit.

His essence is a delicious blend of tart and salty. I want to taste more of it. More self-conscious than I've been since the first time I sucked dick, I carefully pull him into my mouth. I can't throat him the way does but my tongue has a trick or two as I swirl up and over the rim of his head. Unless he's faking, he seems to be satisfied with my amateurish skills.

Once he starts thrusting, I pull off, leaving his tip with a soft kiss. "I want you inside me."

Caleb is looking right into my eyes. "I was inside you."

I flick my tongue out once more to taste him before crawling up beside him. "I want you to fuck me."

Both of his hands cup my cheeks as he kisses me with a passion I've never felt before. Finn was a selfish lover and my few boyfriends before that were mostly closeted and just trying to get off. Caleb is worshipping my mouth in a way that I could get used to. I'm almost disappointed when he finally pulls away but then I remember what's next.

Without waiting for instructions, I roll on to my belly. I'm embarrassed about throwing myself at him when I was in his apartment but it was all real. The drug let me drop my inhibitions but my desire to have him fuck me was as real then as it is now.

Caleb grabs my hips and tugs me up on my knees so he has better access. I'm waiting for a finger or lubed condom to penetrate me but it's Caleb's hot, wet tongue that finally makes contact with my eager hole.

He wraps his arms around both of my thighs and spreads me wider. His tongue has the strength of a nail as it pokes into me. It takes me a second to relax enough that he can squeeze past the rim. With a few gentle thrusts, he slides a finger in below it, making me whimper at the visual in my mind. "Fuck that's good."

Caleb's tongue moves quickly against his finger before pulling it out and sliding in a second finger. His teeth graze my ass as he continues to loosen me up.

Just when I think I'm going to succumb to the euphoria filling my entire being, I feel his thick head lining up with my entrance. "Yes, please do it."

"Eager much?" He laughs as he presses his head fully into me.

"Fuck yeah." I press back until my balls hit his. "Since the minute I saw you."

"Good answer." His thrusts quickly progress from slow and gentle to frantic and rough. Exactly the way I want it. The way I need it.

Caleb holds my hips steady as he enters me from different angles. Sometimes he comes in straight and hard, sometimes he presses to the right, shooting a flare down my spine.

As soon as he knows where to point, he alternates between torture and ecstasy with each thrust. I'm causing a puddle in my sheets but I don't care. Just when I know I can't take much more, Caleb's soft hand wraps around my cock and pumps twice, pulling the orgasm from deep within my core to the ends of each extremity.

My toes curl and my hair tingles as I shoot creamy ribbons onto the bed. "Fuck, Caleb." I'm not sure if I spoke out loud or not but Caleb knows. His fingers dig into my hips as he pushes hard into me. His pulsing dick is releasing as his delicious moans make me hard again.

"God damn." I collapse on the bed with Caleb's weight on my back.

"Yeah." His tongue laps against my shoulder. "We should have done that a long time ago."

~**~

"So you're happy?" Heather and I are watching Pawnography while Charlie Ann naps in her room.

"I am." I take a bite of pizza and contemplate my answer. "I thought I was just lonely before. But since meeting Caleb, I know what it's like to actually be happy. That's super corny but it's true."

"Disgustingly corny." She taps my knee with her socked foot. "But I'm so happy for you. You deserve it."

I shrug. "I don't know about that but I do know that I've never laughed so hard or felt so deeply as I have in the past month."

"So what's next for you guys?"

"I want to ask him to move in." I glance at Heather to see if she has any idea what I'm referring to. Dylan explained that his sister doesn't know anything about the stable he runs above the arcade. When she doesn't seem to catch on, I have to think of a way to carefully word it. "He has a much nicer place than me but…um….I'd like to wake up with him."

She nods and looks out her window. "Yeah, I know what you mean."

I reach out and grab her feet, pulling them onto my lap. "Well, I can't meet all your needs but I'm always here to rub your feet or give you a back massage."

"Oohhh, that feels good." She lays back on the sofa and closes her eyes. "I knew I kept you around for a reason."

~**~

When I pull into the garage to pick up Caleb, he's waiting outside the elevator. It's our one month anniversary and we have reservations at Aquariva.

I pull up beside him and roll down the window. "Hey, sexy. Need a ride?"

He leans in the open window and blatantly checks me out. "I was waiting for my boyfriend but you look pretty good."

When he slides into the passenger seat, I pull his arm so he almost lands in my lap. "I look pretty good?"

He smiles against my mouth. "You're the sexiest man I've ever seen."

"Good answer." I kiss him long and hard, pulling back only when my lungs begin to burn. "God, I've missed you."

"Me too." He nips my lip then sits back in the seat and adjusts his safety belt. "But I'm starving."

"Yes, sir."

As we're waiting at a light, I look over at Caleb's perfect profile. He's drumming his thumb against the door handle to the music and I could just watch him for hours.

"What?" He catches me staring and cocks his head toward me.

"Move in with me."

"Really?" He points to the green light and we start moving again. "Like permanently?"

I grab his hand and pull it to my mouth, leaving a lingering kiss on the back of it. "I hope it's permanent. But at least I'll get to wake up with you every morning and fall asleep with you every night."

He squeezes my fingers and looks out the window. My heart drops as I anticipate his rejection. It's too soon. He would be giving up a luxury apartment at Paddles to move into my little dump. I was both relieved and worried when Caleb explained that with his new job as the financial controller, he could continue to live in the building.

"You sure you want me around all the time?" he asks quietly. "We haven't been together very long. What if you change your mind?"

I pull to the side of the road and cup the back of his neck. "I won't change my mind. And even if one of us does, I'd rather spend every second with you that I can right now than to miss you more often than I see you."

He bites his lip then smiles. "Okay."

"Okay." I wrap my arms around him and slide one palm down to his ass. "Just wait til I get my hands on you tonight."

Read Vinnie's story in
More Than Friends #6: Best Chance

More M/M Romance books by Aria Grace:

More Than Friends series

More Than Friends (#1)*

Drunk in Love (#2)*

Choosing Happy (#3)*

Just Stay (#4)*

Hands On (#5)*

Best Chance (#6)*

My Name is Luka (#7)*

Finally Found (#8)*

Hands On

Looking For Home (#9)*

Choosing Us (#10)*

Mile High Romance series

When It's Right (#1)*

When I'm Weak (#2)*

When I'm Lost (#3)*

When You Were Mine (#4)*

When I Fall (#5)*

When Whiskey Stops Working (#6)

Promises Series
(M/M and M/F Contemporary)

Break Me Like a Promise (#1)

Trust Me Like a Promise (#2)

Keep Me Like a Promise (#3)

Real Answers Investigations series

Corner Office (#1)*

Soy Latte (#2)*

Cheers To That (#3)

Standalones

His Undoing (Gay For You)*
Winter Chill (First Time Gay)*
Escaping in Oz (College First Time)
*Also available as an audiobook

If you enjoyed this book, please consider leaving a review. Indie authors need all the support we can get. Thanks so much!

Learn more at www.AriaGraceBooks.com or become a kick ass fan and join my mailing list for updates and free book opportunities.

ariagracebooks@gmail.com

https://twitter.com/AriaGraceBooks

https://www.facebook.com/ariagracebooks

http://youtube.com/ariagracebooks

http://www.amazon.com/author/ariagrace

AN EXCERPT OF BEST CHANCE BY ARIA GRACE

CHAPTER ONE

VINNIE

"Can I get a Dry Manhattan?"

I look up at the unfamiliar face sitting across the bar and smile. "Sure thing."

I've been working at Ray's for almost five years and most of the patrons are regulars but we get a few strangers in every night. He seems to be one of those strangers. But, he's pretty focused on the game playing above my head so I don't expect any trouble from him.

"Thanks, man," he says without a glance when I slide the glass in front of him. "Just open a tab."

"You got it." I accept the matte blue credit card he slips across the bar and move it to the back counter. "Let me know when you need another."

Despite the game, it's a quiet night. Tuesdays usually are. I'm trying to keep myself busy with an inventory form when I hear a knocking on the bar. New guy is bouncing the corner of his glass against the polished wood.

"Can I get you something?" I ask, standing in front of him again.

"Another." He slides the empty glass to me. "Keep em coming."

Oookaaay. We'll see about that. I pour him another and drop the new glass onto a napkin in front of him. "Here ya go, friend."

His head jerks to mine for the first time. "Friend?"

"Yeah."

"I'm not your friend. I'm your customer." He narrows his eyes as he takes a drink. "You wanna be my friend? Then keep my glass full."

I nod once and walk away. Asshole. There are some empty bottles out on the floor so I take advantage of the lull to bus some tables. We just lost our part time bartender and Ray hasn't found anyone to take up the weekday slack yet. I may have to run an ad myself if it takes much longer.

I'm only gone a few minutes but dude is banging his glass against the bar obnoxiously when I get back. I guess he's ready for another. Without acknowledging his wait, I pour a third Manhattan and slide it in front of him. His eyes flick down from the TV and bore into me. "Thanks."

"Yeah."

I pride myself on being a professional and not easily rattled. I'm willing to let some drunk asshole insult me or otherwise give me shit if it'll keep the peace in the bar. But, something about this guy is seriously rubbing me the wrong way. I know he's just out for a good time like everyone else but if he knocks his glass for me one more time, I might lose my cool.

As if sensing my frustration, Tony wanders over and drops into the seat at the far end of the bar. "Everything cool, bro?"

"Yeah, we're good." I glance over to Mr. Manhattan with a grimace on my face. "This dude's kind of a douche but probably harmless."

Tony gives him a once over and nods. "Yeah, probably."

"How you doing?" I ask the bar manager. He's Ray's right hand man and here almost as often as me. Ray gave him a job as a bouncer when he was twenty and eight years later, the guy hasn't left. He'll probably buy the bar from Ray at some point. Even though he's part of management now, he still uses his 300 pound linebacker build to intimidate customers that get out of hand. "Anything new going on in your life?"

"Nah, you know me." Tony laughs and stretches his dark arms, which are covered in even darker tattoos. "Married to the job. Just wish she was a better cook."

"Yeah, you and me both." I'm laughing on the outside but cringing on the inside. The reality is I'm just as pathetic as he is. I work six or seven days a week behind this bar because I've got nothing better going on in my life. I love Ray and all my regular customers but it's been a long time since I've been with someone that was actually interested in more than a one-night stand or free drinks.

I hear the glass knocking against my bar again and tense up. "I'm going to kill that fucker," I whisper to Tony.

He laughs a deep, booming laugh and stands up. "I'll let you get to it."

I don't know if I should be pleased that he knows I'd never hurt anyone or insulted that he doesn't think I'm capable of it. Because as the knocking becomes more insistent and piercing, I'm mentally searching for the ice pick that I know I left somewhere under the bar.

CHAPTER TWO

CHANCE

"Tomorrow, I promise." Melanie has been riding my ass about taking a night off since we opened the gym two months ago but it's just not possible yet. I've got too much work to catch up on and not enough time to do it during business hours. That leaves very few hours in the day to attempt a social life. Even a pretend social life is overwhelming. "Thursday the latest. I just want to get the new members in the system before morning."

"No." She wedges her five foot nothing body in front of the computer keyboard so I can't see it or the monitor. "I told you I'd do that. Now get your ass out of here."

"You're seriously insisting on this?" I blow out a deep breath and lace my fingers behind my neck as I sit back in my chair. "Why now? Why tonight?"

"It's been long enough, Chance." She places both of her palms on my outer thighs and gives me a little squeeze. "You need to start living again. For all of us."

"Soon, okay." I turn away from her critical gaze. I know she's counting the new lines around my eyes. It seems like there's a new one every day. And then those damn greys around my temple that I just noticed a few days ago. I shouldn't feel so fucking old at twenty-six.

"Tonight," she insists. "I've got everything covered. Carter and I are watching movies and eating popcorn until we puke and you are going out."

"You know he can't eat popcorn." I raise an eyebrow to her. Of course she knows that. She's just as aware of his limits and restrictions as I am.

"I'm kidding, you idiot." She grabs me by my elbows and pulls until I'm standing. "Just go. We'll be fine."

"If I go tonight, do you promise to leave me alone for the next six months?"

She barks out a laugh. "Six days, definitely. Six weeks, doubtful. Six months...just get your ass out of here before I call you an escort."

My business partner is just obnoxious enough to actually do it so I step into the locker room for a shower. When I emerge twenty minutes later, I'm dressed in casual street clothes. A pair of worn jeans and a Rugby I keep in the back but rarely wear. I usually stay in cotton shorts and t-shirts when I'm at the gym. There's no one I'm trying to impress.

With a triumphant smile, Melanie gives me a kiss on the cheek and a pat on the ass as I walk out the front door. "Hope you get laid," she calls as I lock the door behind me.

"Glad you're not," I mumble to myself as I walk to my car.

Now that I've agreed to go out, I have no idea where to go. How pathetic is that? I grew up in Portland and knew this town like the back of my hand at one point. But that was a long time ago. It feels like a lifetime ago.

Without putting too much thought into it, I get in the car and start driving. The downtown bars are always packed, even on a Tuesday night, so I turn down some backstreets and come across a hole-in-the-wall billiards joint I've heard of a few times.

Ray's doesn't look like much from the outside but if they sell beer, that'll be good enough to get Mel off my ass for a while.

~**~

When I first walk in, the large space is almost intimidating. There are only a few people scattered at tables throughout and one guy sitting at the bar. Since I don't want to draw attention to myself by sitting alone at a table in the empty room, I head straight to the bar and take a seat two stools away from the other guy.

He's watching the game on a screen hanging from the ceiling but the way he's rapping his empty glass against the countertop makes me think he's already had a few.

"I'll be right with you," the bartender says quietly as he passes in front of me to deal with the other customer.

"How about a cup of coffee, man?" the bartender says to the guy.

"If I wanted a fucking cup of coffee, I'd be at Starbucks." He thrusts the glass across the bar. It slides right off the back but the bartender grabs it mid-air. "Another Manhattan, *please*."

"I'm sorry, buddy but I can't keep serving you." He pulls out a bottle of water. "Finish this then if you want another drink after that, we'll talk."

My eyes are glued to the drunk man sitting near me. I can't tell if he's actually drunk or just being an ass. After watching him for another minute, I decide a definite asshole vibe is flowing off him in waves.

"Okay, Mom." He grabs the bottle and finishes it in one breath. "Now I gotta pee."

He stands dramatically and takes a second to steady himself on his feet. "When I get back, I'll have a double."

"I'll have a single and a cab ready for you when you get back," the bartender says. His voice is steady and firm as he stares down the guy.

I keep my eyes on the dude as he stands as tall as he can and walks to the back of the bar.

With a shake of my head, I look to the bartender and smile. "Giving you a hard time?"

"He just doesn't know when to say when." He laughs and walks to me. "What can I get you?"

I finally look at the man and instantly recognize him. "Vinnie? Vinnie Brady?"

The bartender flinches at his name and squints a little, tilting his head to really look at me. It only takes a moment for a broad smile to cover his face. "Chance Bodin. Where the hell have you been, man?"

I reach across the bar and grasp his hand tightly, looking into those chocolate brown eyes I've thought about so many times over the past ten years. Has it actually been that long? "Well, you know, did the college thing...then got married."

Vinnie smiles and nods while he pulls out a frosty mug.

"Beer?" he asks, pointing to each tap. When he gets to Pallet Jack IPA, I nod. "Yeah, congrats. I heard you got married. That same girl from school?"

I can feel my face burning at the mention of high school. That's when I met Vinnie for the first time. And when I fell in love...with a boy. We spent a confusing summer together before our senior year. It was the best and worst three months of my life. But, when school started that fall, I pretended like it never happened and hooked up with the prettiest cheerleader on the squad. Then I married her.

"Yup, Katie Wilson." I grab the mug he sets in front of me and take a long draw, searching for the words that will make this moment less awkward. When none come to me, I just accept it for what it is. The story of a coward that was too afraid of what people might say about him to be honest with himself. "We went to school together in Washington then got married. I just moved back last year."

"Wow," Vinnie says slowly. "Good for you man. That's great."

"Yeah, thanks." I take another swig of my beer, unable to make eye contact with him. "What about you?"

Vinnie glances at the drunk guy who's approaching his stool.

The guy seems to have sobered up a bit after his piss. "I'll take that last drink then you can cash me out."

Vinnie pours a drink that I can tell is more vermouth than bourbon and slides it to him before he turns to the register. As soon as the receipt is printed, Vinnie drops it in front of the guy and returns his attention to me.

"Sorry about that," he says quietly. "I just want to get him out of here before he gets out of hand."

"No problem." I nod and take another drink of my beer. "You were about to tell me what you've been doing for the past...what's it been, eight years?"

Read more of Vinnie and Chance's story in

More Than Friends #6: Best Chance

Made in the USA
Middletown, DE
23 November 2024

65272199R00149